The Words We Use are Black and White

Simon Holloway

Safkhet
Publishing

First published in 2014 by Safkhet Select, Wilhelmshaven, Germany
Safkhet Select is an imprint of Safkhet Publishing GbR
www.safkhetpublishing.com

ISBN 978-3-945651-01-8

Printed and bound by Lightning Source International

Typeset in Crimson with Adobe InDesign

Meet Simon on Facebook at https://www.facebook.com/SimonHollowayWriter
or connect with him on Twitter @SimonJHolloway and check out his blog at
http://sjholloway.wordpress.com/

Kim Maya Sutton   *copy editor*
Sally Neuhaus   *cover designer*
Simon Holloway   *author*
Walter Richardson   *proofreader*
William Banks Sutton   *managing editor*

The colophon of Safkhet is a representation of the ancient Egyptian goddess of
wisdom and knowledge, who is credited with inventing writing.
Safkhet Publishing is named after her because the founders met in Egypt.

XHF and RJH

1
Evian

Lucy sells tickets at the weekend cinema. Once the film has started she counts and separates the takings, restocks the snack machines, is able to hear distant shouts or rumbles from the auditorium. Even before the last of the audience has left she helps to sweep the rows of seats and clear the litter.

At the airport schools of immigrant workers move in shifts through the hours, teams of cleaners dispersing through arrivals and departures, meeting, crossing, moving. Their yellow fluorescent jackets mark them out, allow them dispensation to breach lines of passengers or restriction. A few, chosen carefully, wear an extra badge to get into secure areas. Two ride on carts, seeping liquid beneath them and scooping it up from the plastic, slip-proof floor. Lucy sees them sometimes as they pass the all-night café.

She likes the café at night, goes there when the beautiful quiet of the lake becomes breathless. Not often, no, and her visits are not regular. But she will drift from the small cinema with its back to the water, stand with a cigarette and the rasping air, and realise that she wants that other quiet. The lake edge of Geneva is faceless. She doesn't see it as she drives through, although she knows it is there. Stripes of blank buildings line the town, an upper-case neon sign on each roof. She passes on towards the airport avoiding the glare, that conglomerate of invisibility which has coated the city to make it any city, every city, while behind and away Geneva lurks. She can hear it waiting, chuckling, busy. In the café she rests with her quiet.

By eleven o'clock there are bags of rubbish stretched like lost luggage in front of the check-in desks. They lie ignored against the grey, textured plastic. At five they are still there. Manes sees them on his break, as he sees them each night on a walk outside to the terminal's paved approach to fill his blood with unpurified air. Morning comes late in the thinning cross-border mist. Behind him the Jura Mountains hide the sun, in front of him a field of other distant mountains drown him, like the heavy green steppes of Darjeeling never did to his grandparents. His minutes click away, until he turns to the endless sweep of the automatic doors and walks back to the slow growls of his floor sweeper.

Evian suits her. It is seasonal, changing, welcomes different tenses of clientèle, the casino crowds, the walkers and skiers, the old who sit by the lake, the fashionable from Dijon. Close to the elegance and the finery three good restaurants can still see the angled crash of the roof over the pizzeria. It has hung there forever, functioning to its ancient, modern design. Rain is able to fall on three tables. The tourists use them before they take the back road down to the shore, past the supermarket and the laundrette, to watch the casino staff greet their guests. The boat from Lausanne sounds its horn four times. Eight minutes to arrival, twenty-three until the film is supposed to start, Thursdays, Fridays, Saturdays. On Sunday there is no show, out of respect for the town.

Evian suits her. In the winter she slithers to the foot of the slopes, watches the breaths of skiers billow and rage. She skied in Colorado once. The faces there wore different laughs behind their goggles. As evening collapses on Châtel and Morgins the roads will spill with figures entering and leaving bars or restaurants, rotating, the sweet sweat of kir like a shared word, boots tamping clear on the doorways. The noise will distract and perforate. Lucy can return to her second-floor apartment, facing away from the lake, four streets away. She has a balcony to stand on, too small for a table. Instead she hangs washing, keeps a Japanese Painted Fern in a brown pot. She has cheese, giant tomatoes which last her three days, books, four pairs of sunglasses. When the sunlight catches the arrays of spa-water tourists she wishes she had something to regret.

Up above the lake, on the winding, cambered roads across the shallower hills, jubilant trees spill in contained woods. They grow tall and close, pack the partitioned land and shield the road in shadow, dark and treacherous, ice-traps were it not for the slope of the tarmac. Those stretches are the only respite from snow, a bleak and welcoming blast against the mounds to the side. Stakes driven into the ground mark the edge of the road, small spindles before the ditch. Lucy has walked there, forced her wide feet into strong boots and paced back and forth between the firs. Her ankles stretch against the slope. She leans into it, hears the ice cracking in high, desperate branches. Once she wore a yellow hat, pulled down over her ears. It was late April in a year when Easter was early, and the few people she saw as she switched to and fro on the walk from her apartment all wore bright colours. She pushed the hat to the back of the second drawer down when she got home. The lights were already on along the waterfront. Traffic surged from the shore road below the hospital and all along the high route from Amphion and Thonon, avoiding the scourge of the town.

In spring and summer she can smell the water factory. She knows the air, the direction of the Genevese winds, has learnt to tell the

2

difference between the ripples on the lake, the mountains around her and the city to the west, industrial, wealthy and eager. Until she was twenty-two she could not differentiate, felt a single mass of scents throughout the year. The water, hills, town and city all joined in a unified, everyday Evian, even with the restaurants and the pizzas swimming in hot, swamped August evenings. On her balcony she would lean against the railing and read, budget editions of classics, Balzac, Gide, de Beauvoir, tasting the heavy-lined coats and cut clothes of the hotel above the casino.

The seats at the café are green, the rich, swollen jade of ripe tea bushes. Lucy clicks the lid loose on her disposable cup, beckons the scent to her with the tips of her fingers. The table is almost at the right height for her. She tenses the muscles of her thighs to feel them move, watches the messages of their shapes rise and form. A cricket leaps by her feet. The air around her whispers into her coffee smell, antiseptic, filtered, full of the night cleaning fluids, floor degreasant. A trolley is pushed by, its yellow sack bulging with discarded travel essentials. The sombre woman at its command bends to retrieve an empty sandwich wrapper. Her hips creak as she returns to her leaning position, how many hours left in the clean walkways, a distance from ending, spare wishes in her tired eyes of hope, travel, a beginning with and for her children. The wheels of the trolley make no sound. Lucy waits for her to move on, sees the wide rolling of her body merge into the cream walls and grey floor, lights in every colour at the closed car-rental desks. The brown cricket bounds on. Cages of new newspapers are appearing outside closed shops. Soon passengers will begin to thrill the terminal with promise and destination. It is safe for Lucy to leave now, before the hum of the air conditioning disappears into the next daily parades.

The lake is clear. At its edge you can see small catfish and perch flit about in the shallows, praying for bands of well-wishers to cast out yesterday's bread. When she was young Lucy hung chicken skin on string and enticed crabs to cling on, pulling them clear of the water and into her blue bucket. They would crawl over each other slowly, a living, changing mound, until the bigger ones were left at the bottom and clawed at the preying sunlight with waving, slow-motion urgent pincers. When she poured them back into the water they sank together. Her favourite moments, all the effort, to watch them disentangle and head off gently for scraps at the bottom edges of rocks.

She is tall, as tall as you would think if you saw her sitting behind the counter at the cinema. She slides tickets across and chants prices, calculates change. You do not see her behind the perforated glass. Manes thinks he wants to wave at her when he sees her in the sharper air outside the airport, or should at least acknowledge that he recognises her from other nights. Fabrice tries to talk to her under the cinema's porch in the spare passage of the film, slowly at first, words appearing like colours when the light begins to last over the lake in the spring. The water is gentle and diffident, somehow impassioned. If the mists stay high in the mountains you can see across to Lausanne.

As she watches or waits for her brother at the ski runs the children rush towards her, streams of colour ploughing as they have been taught, knees slightly bent, loose, an amiable willingness in their hips to flex and swirl. Behind the weaves of children comes their guide, a school-teacher or activity leader, perhaps a practised parent for the smaller groups, a smile as they pass Lucy and leap to a stop, no eye contact when they shuffle across to the lift near where she stands, watching. She is wearing a jumper and her dark green trousers, thick cotton. They are not the clothes of a skier. When Jean-Luc arrives she will ski.

Near the foot of an intermediate slope three boys rake to a stop, easily, complacent with youth. The last one switches the pole in his right hand to his left.

"It's like it was in February," he says. The deep, vivid red of his jacket lights the snow around him. He is nine, perhaps eleven.

The first glances up the hill. A small crash of snow and ice falls from his lower ski. "Last week was colder." He digs at the softening crust with a white pole. "It's too late now."

"No, we'll get another month. You'll see. It'll get cold again, my father said."

"He's just saying that." The middle one drags his hat clear, rubs his long, brown hair free from the sweat of the run. "He tells you whatever he has to, just to keep you happy."

"No he doesn't."

The first skier pulls his pole out of the snow, leans forward as if to push himself off. "Are we going again?"

"I'm telling you, he doesn't." A sparkle of white hair sneaks out at his fringe. "I've got to be home by four."

The second slides away. "Bye then."

"Yes, bye," chants the first. He eases across the last of the slope, towards the drag lift.

"Hey, wait for me." The last switches his pole back to his right hand, grabs at his goggles. He moves through their tracks, deepening

4

in the sunlight. Lucy imagines that one day it will be Richard skiing with his friends while she watches and attends.

In the summer Jean-Luc swam across the lake without realising what he was doing, an instant unmade decision without aim or consequence. The afternoon was one of those bright, hazy ones, spare clouds dappling the sun onto the surface in shifting colours. He was in the outdoor annexe to the pool, lifted himself over the rope and marker buoys and struck out. His arms felt full, he remembers. They wanted to pull him on, bursts and blisters of energy, expressions perhaps of a fervent youth or its ending, sunlight and the summer, Evian. He looked back to see how far he had gone and the town was a bobbing spill in the distance, climbing up towards trees and hills. Lausanne was closer, an achievement, and he knew that before long the high ring of peaks would begin to send shadows and chill.

He had no money for the ferry back across the lake and had to convince the ticket seller that someone would pay for him when the boat docked. Even then he was made to stand on deck rather than go into the cabin. Evening rushed after the lowering sun. The cold and wind made him feel more exhausted than he was, and his shoulders began to ache.

At the quay a small crowd was watching the boat arrive, some to take it back to Lausanne and some to greet the fool at the front, shivering in his swimming shorts. A breeze blew Lucy's hair over her eyes each time she swept it clear. She waited for the curious and the knowing to welcome her brother, then stepped to pay his fare, gave him her jumper and walked away towards the cinema. She thinks she saw Fabrice there, shaking Jean-Luc by the shoulders, laughing, slapping his face and saying "What were you doing?", but she can't be sure.

Richard was born two and a half years later. He was skiing by the time he was three, held between his parents' hands on the nurseries. On the coldest days Lucy skis with them all for a while, then seats herself next to Jean for the long, swaying ride to the cloudline and a crackling rush on the ridges of a black run, savage and freeing. The morning is over and the snow is becoming emptier. Tourists have settled in the hill cafés and restaurants, congratulating themselves. School parties have gone back to their dormitory accommodation to prepare for their afternoons of cultural activity. Jean-Luc and Lucy ski together, almost side by side, cutting into the turns. They know where the ice will be smooth, where the ruts will rattle their knees.

Cristina is Italian, prone to passivity. She stands with Richard near the counter of the dark, wooden café at the bottom of the

5

lift, waiting for Astrid to talk to her. There is a lunchtime queue, as predictable and unhelpful as the confusions of speech from the filling tables behind her. Astrid is short, without stepping back can barely see over the till to serve the next customer, a man whose skin leans towards her, threatening as he looks down, amber, rich, smooth. There are no hints that he has shaved that morning, no marks or scrapes, no remnants of stubble, yet the shades at the corners of his jaw and on his chin tell Astrid that he shaves every day. She glances up to his almond-skin eyes, puts a slice of chocolate cake on the counter, a biscotti, and in her eagerness to move his dread away she spills his coffee into the saucer and has to make him another. Cristina waits patiently, motionless, Richard clinging to his tiredness and her leg.

2
Evian II

Fabrice loved Toronto. Even at the airport he was aware of its variety, the accents surging at him, languages, dialects. In Evian he heard different voices, American, German, Italian, English, Dutch, but they were all stressed with the same tourist flows and intonations. When he was offered the chance to complete his research overseas he had considered Scotland and Belarus, but chose Canada for the ease of communication. He still has friends there, mentions in emails the orange cabs, green and orange, red and orange. If he was in charge of organising transport downtown he always picked the black and orange, liking their implications of acceleration, a sting.

There were other colours, the ubiquitous black, silver, a strange pale blue and white combination which did not seem to belong, but it is the orange which Fabrice remembers. They would spend evenings by the lake, he and his friends, moving from one expensive bar to another, ending up always at Liberté where the girls formed into groups of three or four and drank bottled beer while they talked. He heard everything at Liberté, social news in Spanish or Hindi, Danish, Australian, Mandarin, gossip in the background in Eastern European languages he couldn't place, Croat possibly, Romanian or Slovak, and all underpinned by that relaxed Canadian slide, such a distance from American invective.

Lucy thinks Cristina's legs are too thin. She is envious of her cleavage, would like the simple, uncluttered messages of femininity it conveys, although she would not want the inconvenience of anything other than her own breasts, the attention to clothing, the comfort necessity of underwear. For Lucy, a tight vest and a jumper is a routine, uncomplicated, thoughtless. But Cristina's legs are too thin. Richard wraps himself tightly to her, his arms cherishing, curling around her thigh to touch his own shoulders. Astrid turns with a replacement cup of coffee, frowns and shakes the light hair swishing on her forehead, an automatic disclaimer. She glances up to his jaw line, up to brutal brown eyes.

"Thank you," he says, and lifts the cup onto his tray. Two small forkfuls of the chocolate cake are gone. Next to his plate is a half-crumpled serviette, stained brown. As he lifts his tray the biscotti slides across its plate and tilts onto the used wood, pivots there until he settles at the only empty table.

"Did you see his eyes?" Astrid asks Cristina, wiping a cloth across the counter. Cristina doesn't reply, reaches down and strokes Richard's head, but the child is asleep, clutched upright to his mother's thin leg. Outside Jean-Luc and Lucy catch their edges on a turn, fight the urge to collapse their knees and give to the ice, a crafted strain thumping deep in the femurs of their inside legs as they push on through the bite of the turn. They are below the tree line. It is fast and cold, like morning.

The shops in Evian are designed to confuse, a welcoming strip of fashion, postcards and delicate eat-in pâtisseries for the visitors, stubborn essentials for the residents mingled in, cheap clothes, pharmacies, banks. Lucy drives to the budget supermarket near Amphion, past the west end of the town, past the casino hotel and the swimming pool. If she were to go further she would see the metallic plumes of the water factory, bottles for tables in unknown countries. Or further still the chains of advertised stores, shoes, furniture, electricals, neon restaurants, the hypermarket squinting from a roundabout, but she needs only washing powder, milk and chocolate, a few vegetables, maybe some frozen chicken. Worth the trip to Amphion, but no further.

The road is filled with flowers, every kerb and junction daubed with planned pictures in the blooms, the town name, the lake, fictions of trees and culture. Lucy likes flowers, hears their colours as she curls around them, pauses to look when she gets out of the car even though she has seen them many times before. Once she saw Fabrice carrying two large bunches rolled into one. He was walking away from the cinema, past the travel agents selling boat trips and towards the marina and the newer, wider apartments. It was early afternoon. His shadow was hidden by the old spa. She wondered where he was going, lit a cigarette and called out to him, but he waved a reply and kept walking, behind him the stone and latticed windows growling an echo. When he turned at the corner and began to climb in the direction of the hospital she was happy and sad.

Alain holds his biscotti in the coffee, letting the liquid ease up into the biscuit, permeating, softening. Cristina sits in the spare chairs across from him, lifts Richard onto her lap and cradles him while he wakes up.

She looks briefly to Alain's ferocious eyes, hard and set. "I don't want to talk."

"Then don't." His voice is low and volatile, like a balladeer reciting prose at a funeral.

8

In front of the airport doors Manes is pacing, stirring through the flow of passengers arriving to depart, coaches and taxis producing more and more. The wheels of suitcases rabble on the paving slabs. He is halfway through a day shift, the luxury of light.

"Talking is unnecessary," Cristina says, tearing a packet of sugar open with her teeth. "And you wouldn't hear me even if I did."

"Why not?"

"Because I'm Italian. My accent is difficult."

"I heard that."

She shakes her head to refute his claim. "I don't want to talk."

He lifts the wet end of the biscotti to his lips, lets the drops of infected coffee fall onto his tongue. In ten minutes it is gone, along with more mouthfuls of cake. Two crumpled serviettes rest on his tray.

Richard wriggles to upright, or as close as he can to upright in the restrictions of his mother's care. She holds a glass of milk to him, aiming the yellow straws at his mouth, then hands him a torn piece of sweet, cinnamon pastry. He chews slowly, aimlessly.

At the door of the café a procession is always in progress between eight and three. Skiers stand their equipment in the racks, loosen their boots and stamp inside. Watchers tighten their coats, slide on sunglasses or goggles for the snowblindness as they leave. Between seven and four Astrid watches them, serves them, cleans up after them, on weekends helped by Martine or Beatrice, earning their lift passes. She looks at her watch as she fills the dishwasher, wipes trays, removes a gateau and a half from the freezer for the next day. It is quarter to two. Almost there, almost time to fill the mop bucket, sweep, clean down the coffee machine. A strip light in the display hums and she notes its details down in the maintenance book for M. Guillard, turns the background radio up to cover the interfering noise. An advertisement for a sale at a home improvement warehouse rebounds from the shelf by the radio, branches at Annemasse, Annecy and Thonon, every day this week including Sunday. Her parents would not approve.

Jean-Luc and Lucy have slipped into the low slopes, breathe hard as they glide in the respite through the small children and tourists. They free their bindings and slot their skis and poles into the wooden racks outside the café, pull off their hats and gloves, open their clothes to the sweaty air around them. Luc buys hot chocolate for himself, Sprite for Lucy, and sits next to Alain, making him shift along the table and move his black rucksack to the floor. Alain's eyes are unapologetic, Luc sees, even when he says "thank you".

"She will not talk," Alain recites, depositing a third smeared serviette and his fork on the tray.

Richard holds out a tangled chunk of pastry. "I saved it for you, Papa."

In Toronto Fabrice slipped always into English, his first words to a stranger defining him as an Anglophile, one of the body able to converse with all, secure, global. Small groups would chatter, couples or families, circles, acquaintances, and theirs were the languages he heard accommodated, or more than that, welcomed, into the organism of the city. Yet each time he sat in the front seat of a black and orange cab he chose English, knew as he did so that the driver's first language was almost always other. Eventually he and his friends discarded French altogether. When he landed back at Geneva he had to accustom himself again to the vowel sounds, reform his ears and tongue to their creation. When he speaks English to the tourists at the cinema they think he is Canadian, Québécois, and the Americans hear his closeness and the separation.

The radio plays Brel, *On n'oublie rien*. Lucy adores Brel, the ugliness of his teeth, forging sweat compelling in each note as it surges from his desperate throat. His hair clings to his head, drops flail at the microphone in the black and white footage, arms flailing the words, a certain strain of discourse as if he cannot squeeze the phrases he needs, never accurate enough, missing, slightly to the left or to the right, moments in front of him and almost in reach. Alain watches her sit down, sees the marks of drying sweat on her temples, her tight skin around her eyes and nose, the colour returning to her naked lips. She opens her can of Sprite and drinks, leans to kiss Richard.

"Have you finished skiing now?"

"Yes, Richard."

The boy swivels his head to look up at Cristina. "Can we go home?"

Cristina looks back at him for a few seconds, then kisses his forehead.

"We'll go soon," says Jean-Luc, "once I've finished this." He stirs his hot chocolate, lifting the froth clear then plunging it back into the cup. Twice his elbow bumps into Alain's arm. Alain slides closer to the window and watches Lucy's reflection appear and disappear as the light flickers with distant trees.

Lucy sees Cristina's hair rest against Richard's head as she bows forwards. She likes Cristina's hair, its careful, cultured loops, swirls of night as black as a hanging silence. Gypsy hair, Luc had said,

10

when he first met her on the farthest runs. It took him a year to catch her, or be caught, a season of hard crusts and cold ice. She was back the following winter, fluorescent red ski poles leaning against the window of another, more distant respite. Her hair, he reported back, gypsy, and teeth which could crush you in their smile.

Her legs are too thin, and inelegant. "She walks like a chamois," Lucy said. "You could imagine her clattering over the rocks in the spring, looking for purchase and new growth. I like her, Luc."

"Good."

"Where was she?"

"Cavaglià, on the Italian side of the mountains. Her father creates letters."

"Letters?"

"Digital ones, fonts."

"How did you find her?"

"I don't know. I looked, and she was there."

"Will you bring her with you on Sunday? Mama will want to meet her, at last."

"She doesn't like chatter. Her parents' house is quiet, 'concentrated', she says."

In her absence he had swum the lake for her. Lucy knew that, had seen him striking away from Evian in the rhythmical flow of his heartbeat. She saw many things. When the boat was making its last trip in the summer darkness its third to last lightbulb was not working, a visible gap in the yellow line between mast and prow, as if it was failing to deliver a message. She saw the exhausts of expensive cars flick small sparks on the speed bumps in the hotel car park. Potential customers read the menus outside the three restaurants near the post office, each lunch or dinner guest able to hear only the music of the restaurant behind them, never the one in front. She watched queues form at the ice cream sellers' windows, then walked past them into the shop to be served immediately, or saw the school children stroll past the lunch-closed shops on their way home.

At the small supermarket she listened to arguments about weight or fat content, half a kilo, cut that off, would lie on her bed to the sounds of afternoon couples squabbling in other apartments, then close the shutters and sleep, the water three buildings behind her silent, tideless. When she woke she saw herself, in the late shadows her reflection gleaming at her, a good nose, small, symmetrical, eyebrows always needing care, her short hair bed-worn but never right, never that perfect waking hair she saw from the back of the cinema on the few occasions she crept in, last, to watch moments

11

of that week's film. She was almost proud of her mouth. It was a mouth to be proud of, her father's, wide and curving upwards at the sides in a perpetual state of alertness, apart from the small scar on the lower left side where she had fallen on gravel, an arc of tissue so small as to be not even noticeable. She curled in her bottom lip and raked her teeth over the lifeless skin, enjoying the lack of sensation as her nerveless teeth met the nerveless flesh. But her hair, the cut, brown strands rummaged together by her pillow, nearly elegant, almost graceful or erotic. 'Cristina has beautiful hair,' she thinks, 'I will talk to her.'

Brel sweats from the radio. "Excuse me," Alain says. He sighs and angles to move, leaves his tray on the table as Luc shifts to let him pass. "Thanks," he murmurs, looking at the damp patch on Lucy's elbow where she leant against the ski rack to loosen her boots. She still has her ski jacket on. It is cold in the café, the outside chill rushing in whenever the door is opened, in spite of the sunlight and the heated air being pushed around the ceiling. "Your sleeve is wet," Alain says, pointing to the darker patch.

Lucy rotates her arm. "It's nothing." She flicks the ring-pull of her Sprite with her thumb and it clangs against the Brel. A strand of ski sweat clambers down her neck.

"Your friend doesn't like talking. She told me so." He smiles at her, a balladeer's smile. "Thank you for listening to me." He walks to the door, sending shovels of cold back to their table as he stands with the door open, buttoning his coat.

Richard whines again that he wants to go home and Luc agrees to his request, the fresh wind on the back of his head making him lean to the last comfort of his chocolate. Cristina loosens her grip on the invigorated child and allows the eagerness to slip from her lap to the floor, where he crawls out and across to the counter, picking bags of sugar and forks from Astrid's attention. She shakes the light hair across her forehead. The sweat on Lucy's neck is invigorating and decisive, holds the rushes of exertion. She lights a cigarette as they reclaim their skis, holds her poles and skis in one hand as they crunch to the car park, draws the soothing, silencing smoke into her mouth.

"Fiat," mutters Cristina. They pause to let Alain's car pass by the end of the path. A queue of six cars is already waiting to leave.

Lucy sees the airport at night, the beckoning quiet to follow the cinema-goers. She will read one of the papers on the rack at the all-night café, balance in the depths of a tea green chair and allow the words to soak through her, the news, the articles, pages of medical breakthroughs and earthquakes, the obituaries and the needless squalls of sport. She will consume the details in the business section, the financial reports and company accounts jumbled in insensible necessities, move through to the advertisements, jobs and holidays, the television guide for the evening before, previews, recommendations. She will repeat sentences to herself, aligning phrases, adjectives, reading and announcing the importance of it all.

By three o'clock she will have returned the paper to the rack, need a different view to cool the tremors in her eyes from the graining, classified lights of the terminal. There will be no traffic then, a far-off resonance of travel from the city and its constancy but nothing at Departures. Frost will be shaping on the approaches. Geneva will be somewhere else, an insignia of street lights, able to be located yet other, away, like Evian. She will not hear it in the newsprint scattering in her brain, the cold air, breath like the cigarette she will hold as she speaks.

Alain almost waves from his car as they wait at the cracked end of the path, its breach at the car park tarmac. He reaches instead for the volume control on his radio, the news.

"He talked funny," Richard says, watching the Fiat join the back of the queue.

"He's from the north." A gaze of the cold air is lighting on Cristina's cheeks, as if she was the one who had expelled energy on the hill.

"Where?"

"North," Luc repeats, as if the answer should be precise enough.

"Yes, but where? His words didn't sound right."

Lucy looks back to the café, once. She had not heard his accent in his prose, words willowing from his throat, the low, slow ramble of 'your friend doesn't like talking' making her think of Cristina as a mediaeval heroine, the forlorn love of a troubadour patrolling the Berry countryside around Montluçon. Lucy had summered there with her parents when she was young, strolled bored through the fortress not hearing the history lessons. Nearby were the shops, another language.

"North of Paris, certainly," Luc says comfortingly, lifting Richard into the air to swing him into the car. "Belgium, perhaps, the Ardennes."

Cristina is walking around to open the boot and slide Luc's skis inside the wide depths. "No," she says. She knows voices, can tell even from the most guttural sound whether someone is Dutch,

German or Austrian, separates Greeks, Cypriots and Turks in their breathing. "Industrial north, probably Lille." She stands aside to let Lucy rest her poles in the car, then needlessly adds "Hellemes," to reinforce her assessment.

3
Manitoba

The streets smell of flowers and bread. Morning bakeries send knowledge of their labours through open doors, shoals of Easter tourists filling the avenue of shops as they take a break from the heat of the water's edge, protection in the aromas which draw them, crabs to chicken skin. Fabrice clambers through their current, descending the slope back to the tarmac on his way to visit his grandmother. She cannot see him clearly now, recognises his shape as he draws the blinds of her room, knows him by the sweet cleanness of the roses in his silhouette.

"Doudou," she says from the support of her pillows, cautiously arranged to stop her slipping back down the bed. "You are a good boy now, Doudou, to have come back to see me." She does not mean back again, almost daily, but back from Toronto, the continuous reproach of his work.

"How are you today, Maman Sulpice? Your eyes are shining. You must have slept well," Fabrice replies, answering his own question.

She curls her hand behind her ear, forms a shell to echo his words into her. "I did sleep. I can remember being asleep." The skin of her bent elbow hangs from the bone, loose and translucent in the light angling from the blind. She cannot see Fabrice staring at its pinkness, at the blood pulsing through used veins.

"Your flowers give you away," she says, and lets her eyelids fall to take in the familiar scent.

"I'll ask a nurse to change them for you." He feels he should sit down, make audible signals that he is not anxious to leave. The light leaves her elbow as she releases the effort, skin turning to blue, grey, pink.

"It's easy to sleep, Doudou." She opens her eyes and searches for him, taps the turned sheet next to her to allow him to sit. "Remember this, Fabrice. Sleep is easy."

He knows she is serious, restless. He hears 'Fabrice' and not 'Doudou', tries to listen to what follows and accept her direction, after Toronto and the trees, but he hears 'sleep' and 'Fabrice' and cannot join them together. He smiles for her, an exaggerated show of teeth to show he understands.

"Maman Sulpice, I should have listened to you before."

"Yes, you should."

"I was wrong." He rests the flowers near her feet and covers her exposed hand with his own. "I'm sorry. I should not have gone."

"You made your mother unhappy, Doudou."

"I'm sorry," he repeats. "I didn't know she would be so sad. She didn't tell me."

She flexes her hand under his, touches his palm with her knuckles. "Would you have listened?"

From Toronto he had gone north through Ontario, on to Manitoba and the Riding Mountain National Park to look at the trees. He could have gone to Norway, Finland perhaps, but chose Canada for the language. The deep strength of wood was his life then, eight weeks in a study centre to hear the white spruce and balsam fir breathe. At night he could hear their gasps in the consumptive quiet, sways and sighs not from the wind or the motions of the earth but of their own volition. He lived in their privacy, inured, triumphant. Days of rain or stupefying mists left him engorged.

Each Saturday visitors would leave and arrive, along with tables of supplies for the botanists and ecologists conducting habitat surveys, heavy, waterproof coats and pads wrapped in clear plastic, pens able to withstand the climate. Laptops whirred against the walls of the cabins. Others spoke to him, shared cold beers or hot coffee after dinner, and he spoke back. Accents were easily understood, a cohesion shared in the clearing between the forests, unheard and audible. When he got to the secrecy of his room he wrote or thought in translation, like everyone, accounts of the day, observations, statements to decry or confirm particular points of view, then always a kerosene lamp as the trees held their court, speaking their beliefs.

Alain appeared at the window of the ticket office. It was Thursday, the second showing of an extended run, hot light clinging to the centre of the lake then spiralling slowly away into the circle of mountains. He was carrying a summer jacket folded up under his arm and the sleeves of his shirt were rolled up to his elbows. His left hand was in his pocket, trapping the jacket. The queue in front of him edged forwards, chances to proclaim the same, one, two, a pause as Lucy produces tickets and change, then another pace and a half forwards, another face. He did not emphasise his presence, or hers. His was another face, brutal eyes, a glimpse of hair beginning to break back through his jaw line, one, please, and he left the window and hesitantly walked off towards the auditorium doors. Three girls behind him, almost certainly not old enough to see the film, separated and spread around him, two to his left and one to

16

his right, flowed past him and on. He squeezed his left arm to his body, moved his right hand to protect the security of his jacket, and turned.

At the window a couple were each insisting that they pay for both tickets, an affectation of care. Lucy dragged her top teeth across the blank flesh below her bottom lip, in the moments of the half-hour before the film was due to start enjoying the scene and the action, a hiatus to organise. Alain could see the glass, the man's hand pushing his lover's away and forcing his own in the space. She wore a scarf, green like the algae on the rocks of the lake bed. He watched, the man won his battle and took their tickets, pushed the few coins of change to her in victory, and kissed her cheek. Lucy's shoulder came briefly into view as she leaned to the next in line. Alain saw it, the black of the loose material, wool or a wool-mix, the shape and intonation of the joint beneath it invisible. The queue was longer. He walked to the auditorium.

The carpet is faded red, dulled by so many footfalls that it rests between pink and brown. Paths have been made from the single pair of doors at the entrance to the ticket window and the connecting door at the low wings of the small screen itself, barely able to seat a hundred and fifty, never full. The cinema exists, is subsidised by the town and the tourists for mutual benefit, shows dubbed or subtitled Hollywood films three weeks after the cities, French language films in the spring and autumn. Since Lucy has worked there she has seen more voices and faces come to her than she could imagine existed, their variety, their strangeness, concave eyes through the perforated glass, fingers touching as she takes the money beneath. She may have seen Alain before in other weeks with other films. She may have seen him that day, recognised the colours of his skin or the fraying hair above his temples, the jacket rolled under his arm. When the last of the late had hurried through she walked to the darkening air, watched the ferry with its missing light limp away from Evian. Fabrice was still inside taking tickets, showing the final customers to their seats, and she was alone with a cigarette and the water, ripples slapping secretly against the wall under her. Green and red lights flashed in the distance to her left, a last flight on final approach to Geneva.

Luc and Cristina live above the town, on the flat roads beneath the villages. They bought the house with her father's christening gift to Richard, the rights to a font which has proved far more popular than anyone could have predicted, more profitable than any other he has designed. The font has curved upstrokes, tall, graceful sweeps which resemble the walk and handwriting of a duchess, and its capital letters are wider than usual, giving it an impression of seriousness and importance. Two Italian banks have bought it for their corporate communications. Cristina is negotiating with Vienna and Bratislava to see who will pay the most to have it as their cultural identity.

Richard's bedroom is next to his parents', behind their view to the lake and facing the trees at the top of the garden. Each night Jean-Luc has to perform an incantation before he closes the curtains, Richard sitting up in bed with that night's book at his knees, watching the carefully composed message, no mention of evil or implicit threat:

Creatures of the woodland,
Spirits of the night,
Happy is the darkness,
As happy is the light.
Keep your secrets close to you,
Bring no trouble near,
Sleep safely in your homes tonight,
And we'll sleep safely here.

Luc closes the curtains as Richard repeats the last line, "and we'll sleep safely here" shouted out, a laugh. He shuts his book and bounces to put it on the bookcase, then bounces back to the bed and under the duvet before Luc reaches him.

Cristina is downstairs, watching the fire. She has supervised Richard's bath, sung to him in an Italian dialect he knows only for its comfort, and is now drinking beer, flames from the unnecessary but vital fire reflecting on her bare knees. She is worried about her hair, stilted in the summer breeze, and her car, which has started making menacing, groaning noises as she turns the steep bends by the woods, and about Luc, who has not yet swum in the lake this year even though it has been warm and clear for weeks, almost two months. She lifts her glass of beer to her eyes, sees the bubbles slip their grip and rush to the surface, hears Richard's cry of "and we'll sleep safely here". In a few moments she will hear the click of his light being turned off, a final goodnight, and Luc's soft feet hitting the sides of the treads as he comes quietly downstairs.

The airport empties. Passengers collect their bags and are themselves collected, or trudge to the long-stay car park or bus stops. The airline staff leave and clerks close their desks, "This kiosk is open from 07.00-21.00, at all other times please use the courtesy telephone provided." In their place security guards greet engineers and maintenance crews, tick their names off on the sheets in front of them and release them into controlled zones. In the terminal buildings individuals form into stealthy teams, merge almost invisibly in meeting rooms to receive their instructions and equipment. They spread out into the abandoned halls, into the lost sleepers stretching on benches or across three chairs, and are unseen. As he moves to his duties Manes sneaks through the automatic doors, seeking hourfuls of air, mountainous and placating. He passes two cabin staff as he returns. They have already fastened their night-blue coats for the taxi to the hotel, pull their compact travel cases behind them, talk to each other in German, Manes thinks. One is a woman and one a man. They are the same height, pass him without acknowledgement, but he can tell their genders from the pitch and cadence, off-duty, casual, tired.

"Goodnight," he calls out to their backs, an instinct or politeness.

Their wheels stop. In synchronised motions they turn their heads and smile at him. "Goodnight."

Jean-Luc sits on the sofa, falls against her shoulder and snuffles against the top of her sleeve. He takes in the scents of her, the peculiar, individual languages which make up his wife, soaps, perfumes, fabric softener, the effect her sweat creates in them. A sigh surges into the fawn cotton, an emitted relaxation. He smells the warmth of his own breath, its dampness and vapours.

"Why don't you want to swim?" Cristina asks. Her hair is annoying her. On the corners of the road her car makes malevolent, grating noises near the front wheels.

"I don't know." Luc smells her again, and himself. "It just doesn't occur to me."

"You could take Richard."

"Yes." He closes his eyes. She is warm, compact. "He prefers skiing."

"He's three years old. His favourites are yours and mine. Take him swimming, Jean." She pronounces Luc's name with a harder J, forceful and demonstrative, possessive. "We could all go," she says, in a quiet flurry of compromise.

Jean-Luc lifts his head from the womb of her shoulder, sings a breath as he looks and leans to her exposed cheek. In her glass the bubbles are rising more slowly. He kisses her, lets his lips rest lightly against the skin below her cheekbone, drawing on the last of the foundation left on her day. He is close to her now, close enough to touch.

"You're right," he says, yielding. "He needs to swim. Let's all go, this weekend." He sits up, thinks of standing then changes his mind. "Did you get anywhere today?" he asks, meaning Vienna and Bratislava, the Oregon Banking Association, Arcson Plastics.

"The car's not good. I went towards Martigny and the turns on the way up, the noise. Will you call the garage for me? They don't take me seriously. My accent."

"Of course. I'll do it in the morning."

Alain slides a bag of shopping into the footwell of his car, fearing it will slip off the seat and break the bottle of basil oil. Did he love Lucy? Perhaps he just could not speak the love he had. He used the phrasing, said 'I love you' enough times to convince her, the most apt opportunities, more so at inappropriate times or in the wrong situations, almost as if by expressing the emotion unexpectedly he could instil in it more force.

He doesn't want basil oil on the upholstery or carpets, drives gently to keep the bread and peppers dry, the local Richebourg cheese, a loose packet of ham sliced to his specifications. He has always eaten simply, likes uncomplicated food prepared without worry or precision. He sits happily with ripped, fresh bread and a bag of tomatoes, takes bites from each alternately and chews his delight, putting down half a tomato now and then to rinse his mouth with water or all of a small glass of orange juice, then refills the glass for the next occasion and picks up his tomato. By the time he has finished all the bread he wants his left hand, always his left hand, is soaked in tomato juice and loose seeds. Whenever he can he finishes the meal with yoghurt, uses that same stained hand to hold a large pot while he circles a spoon in his right hand, pot to mouth, repeat, unflavoured, its plainness settling the acid in his throat.

Lucy took him to restaurants, cooked complicated meals for them both to coax an appreciation of subtlety. Though he would follow her example and savour the differences he never altered his passion, and his simple food held a charm which she could not understand. "There's music in these tastes, Oose, can't you hear it?" he said. "A poetry all of its own."

Richard had named her Oose. When he began to speak Luc had moved him from Ma-ma and Pa-Pa to the commanding lake and to Water, which came out as Wa-wa, and Ball, Bor. The letter L contrived problems for Richard's snipped tongue. Eventually he managed to recognise Lucy as Oose, and when she recounted the tale to Alain he took it for her, held her with it. He used it for tenderness or to convey intimate sincerity, whispered 'I love you, Oose' when

20

they were alone, broadcast the same statement louder in public, a declaration.

But no, there is no certainty about his love. She counted up the small actions, added notes to each one, implications, even began to listen intently to the tones of his languid, lulling voice to see behind his lips to the vision inside. In the mornings she watched him shave, moved a chair into the tiny bathroom to get a better sight of his expressions. When he concentrated on the resisting awkwardness of his jaw line she thought she could see an acrid bitterness in his eyes, different from his normal ferocity, but it might have been the freshness of his waking or the anticipation of breakfast.

As to love, she was as certain as she could be. In his words and eyes there could be any meaning she chose, and she had chosen his love. What else could she do? She can only hear the information given to her, take signs, read the shapes of his face like she reads the day-old newspapers at the airport café, the feature articles and business reports, the obituaries, the culture section, repeat sentences to herself in the cold air and find her own responses.

She sees Jean-Luc and Cristina, accepts coloured traces from them, insights. She takes some too from her parents. But her opinions ultimately have to be hers alone. Not even Alain can instruct her on this. He can influence her, smile in that imitation of timidity when he lowers his head and looks up at her, can take her in his arms on the steel frame of her balcony as the quiet street below flashes by, yet he cannot give her an accurate, precise version of his feelings for her, just as she cannot explain herself to him. This is the love she has, given to her and by her. An amalgam of fractured messages, their completeness like a sound you thought you heard, an animal to the side of you in the woods, and when you look it has gone to the cover of the ferns and broken branches, and we'll sleep safely here.

Fabrice left Toronto and headed north, to the wilds of the park and the physicality of his research. As he travelled he forgot the orange cabs and Liberté, carried with him only for the first few hours thoughts of Emily and her basement flat on Charlotte Street, the winter ice creeping under her back door from the outflow pipes of the flats above. The trees held whispers, recollections of other lives, the peace of the lake when he walked along the shore, east from Evian, through the spring dormant villages trapped between the train tracks and the water. He was shown to his room in the fourth cabin, introduced himself to Jean-Christophe and Kennet in the rooms either side of his, to Max and Diane from Wisconsin in the double at the far end, then took his remembrances to the forest floor.

It was raining, he can remember that, slow, fine symbols of rain clouding the clearing. Once he was under the canopies he could take his camera and notebook safely from his bag and watch the world subside. Time passed. He wrote down what he saw, descriptions of the layout and structure of his forest, the density and spread of trees, their interlocking arms reaching always for connection and clear sky, the varieties and growth patterns of mosses, root weaves visible from huge fallen saplings or ancient masters. He took pictures as the days left him, lichens and dying leaves, decay as important as growth, inseparable, colours and contours.

In his third week he was taken, claimed. Max noticed it first, nudged Diane as they all sat to eat in the candid electrical glow of the evening cabin.

"It's got to him," he said.

Diane smiled, the cracked weather of her skin easing to Fabrice's curious, returning stare. "It gets to everyone, sooner or later. Don't worry, honey."

"What does?"

"She's like a lover. She wears you down. We've been coming here now for twelve years, off and on, and we see it all the time."

Fabrice looked down at his plate, at the delicate steamed salmon and potato tostadas. Kennet was the one who cooked, brought Swedish and North American recipes together, appearing in minutes to turn their standard fish or chicken supplies into new creations, cooked passions.

Lucy sells tickets, Cristina worries about her car, Fabrice takes flowers to Maman Sulpice.

He slipped his knife into the silver skin, lifted pale pink flesh onto a splinter of potato, lime juice, lemon juice. "I'm sorry, I don't understand what you mean. What do you see?"

Max looked to his wife, saw her chewing her own display of fish and translated her knowing actions for her. "It's like this, is what I'm saying. You come here for whatever reason, a science project, some conservation program, I don't know, and you bring all your things with you, your books and papers, some complicated research report or other on bio-diversity. A couple of years ago some guys hauled arc lights and blow-heaters so they could disrupt them, and see what happened. They lasted five days. The trees get to you, that's what it is."

22

"They take over," Diane forced out through the fennel and oils.

"They take over. Sometimes it takes a while, but sooner or later everyone just ends up sitting in the quiet, watching them. Unless you're only here for a day or so." Max picked up his Coke, held it loosely at the bottom of the can as he drank. "And it's not some kind of spell. Don't think I'm saying that."

"No magic," Diane reiterated in the space left for her, a discourse repeated each trip, adjusted, practised.

"But it's like Diane was saying, it wears you down. You come here full of aims and aspirations, wanting to learn about the forest, but it takes over. It tells you what it wants, and you don't get to choose."

"She's like a lover. She makes sure you hear what you need to so that you fall for her, and then the forest's got you. All you can do is just be near her, around her, waiting for her to pay attention to you. And it's never enough."

"Never is."

"That's why we've been coming back up here all these years. Sure, it's a long drive, but think what we get in return. We come to visit, and we get to fall in love all over again."

"And not only with the forest." Max squeezed Diane's little finger, let Kennet and Jean-Christophe rest in the refreshed quiet and smiled again at Fabrice, still mired in his salmon.

4
Geneva

Alain's eyes are not brutal or ferocious, of course. They rest in their recesses like everyone else's, waiting for something to cause a response, an image, an inverted refraction, a sound or touch. His eyes move. They shift to the source of attention, react in dilation or contraction, focus, receive and determine. It might be his amber skin, an inheritance of the south, the smooth turns of his mouth, the serrated fraying hair at his temples or the flecks of eyebrows above his nose. Marie told him his eyes were impatient, weeks before she left their house in Geneva.

"You watch me all the time," she said. "You make me feel like you want me to relax, to settle. I've told you, I need to adjust."

"I thought women liked being looked at."

"They do, but you do it so badly," she shouted, slamming closed the doors of the bathroom cabinet.

She stopped making love with him, said she felt like she was being scrutinised in her nakedness. For a month he tried to soften his glances. He kept his eyes lowered to respect her and her wishes, until he returned home from work to the abandoned house and a note slipped silently under the door, 'I've failed your inspection, love, Marie.'

He couldn't reclaim the space as his own. Four months later he emigrated the forty kilometres to Evian and took to learning the language of looking away. He kept the black Fiat for its invisibility, a standard family saloon like any you would see descending from the bottom of ski runs or glancing askance at the lake. After he recognised Lucy in the perforations of the ticket office window he stood far enough away so as not to be seen, saw the cloth at her shoulder move into and out of vision. He has to control himself. For if he is described for others by the shadows of his eyelids, the darkness at his jaw line or the lustre of his skin then that is how he is. Severe. Judgemental. Brutal, perhaps.

And though these definitions are instant and uncalculated they are the ones which will linger, be ghost-like supports for all the subsequent adjectives you could use. He will always be the one with the ferocious eyes. Everything else rests on that understanding, not a first impression but an underlying language of assertions and reasonings. He makes sure the oil does not spill on the way back from the supermarket, eats simple food effortlessly whether alone or not, broadcasting other images, taking his passion seriously. Yet Astrid remembers Cristina waiting at the café, the day the light in the display first began to hum, and thinks how she looked up to see his brutal eyes and smooth skin staring wildly back down at her.

In Evian a wind is carousing the shore of the lake, switching east under the shelter of the mountains and finding itself beating the shop canopies. Postcards are blown from their racks. Newspapers flicker to expose their dainty inside pages, a temptation should anyone be passing. The last few umbrellas stranded in the café tables on the pavement are taken inside in a symbolic act of season. It is almost five o'clock in the afternoon, almost darkening. Lucy has learned slowly that the weeks after summer change quickly, light washing away in minutes from the bowl of the water.

Like most she is indoors. It is Sunday, hours after family lunches to spend rushing to fill the day, shopping at the large, advertised stores past Amphion, cleaning clothes, washing floors, sweeping the balcony of its accumulated autumn. The thin street floor below is carpeted with the mess of other balconies, other apartments, and there is no traffic to clear it away.

There is no showing at the cinema tonight. She would usually pass the discarded evening with dampened sounds, the television, the doors of her wardrobe opening and closing, the hushed, hissed sweep of an iron, the pages of a book turning in dulled sympathy. Later there will be echoes as she lies in the stillness, footsteps above, arguments or snores to the side, until she turns on the radio and falls asleep to its despairing murmurs, hoping for the surprising blisters of Brel and passion to bound to her, his ransomed teeth, his grey sweat.

Yet on this Sunday she showers before six and stares at her reflection in the steam on the mirror. Alain found her again on Thursday, the first night of a new thriller set in Marseille. He waited inside while the smaller queue trailed to her and away, gave her three minutes out under the concrete canopy to light a cigarette before pushing the doors open.

"Excuse me."

She turned to the ballad and the door crashing shut, steel and glass vibrating. Rain traced lines from the canopy to the floor, ancient, undone repairs. She dropped her cigarette to this presence and smeared it into the ground with the sole of her shoe. "I'm sorry, I didn't know you were there."

"No."

"Why don't you just go in? It will already have started. Tell Fabrice I said you could."

"No."

"Go on, tell him I said it's fine, if he asks," she insisted, waving her hand towards the door behind him. "The man at the door," she added, to explain.

"No, I don't want to," Alain began, almost moving, then stopped. In the frame of the rain he could see the wide curve of her mouth. He watched it, thought it was a mouth to be proud of, a mouth he wanted to see speak. She was quiet.

"You spoke to me," he said. "At the café, when your friend didn't want to talk."

"Yes, I remember."

"Thank you."

"For remembering?" She wished she had not thrown down her cigarette so quickly.

"For talking." He stepped closer, felt the rain being blown in over the lake. He held his hand out. "Alain."

She took it, kept her gaze to the steel and glass, the quivering wind. "Lucie."

He was trying not to look at her. She was trying not to look at him. They were trying to speak.

"Sunday," Alain said. He forced himself to watch the rain in the street lights, frowned as if commenting on the weather to disguise the consciousness of his action.

"There's no showing on Sunday."

"No." He looked back to her, looked away again. "Perhaps Sunday is a good evening to eat out, a restaurant, now that they're less crowded."

"I'm normally at home on Sunday." She traded glances at the dark water with him. Fabrice would arrive soon for the ticket money, both of them for safety. "You live here, then?"

"Now, yes. I moved from Geneva."

She forbade herself from smiling at the word, the urge to claim the airport for her own, a good night, a green seat and the newspaper.

"Sunday," he repeated. His right ankle was getting wet, splashes angled under the canopy and through his trousers.

Jean-Luc rang the garage in the morning, passed on Cristina's worries of the malicious growling near the front wheels on hill corners and listened to the list of possible faults. He was waiting for the routine phrases, hard to tell from someone else's descriptions, we'd need to drive it ourselves, and arranged to leave the car with

26

them. Two days later he left early, before Cristina had accompanied Richard to school, handed over the keys and walked the rest of the way to work.

The minutes on the roads outside Thonon soothed, time allowed to pause in the cool hours before the sun came above the hills. He had slept well, a long, deep night with no creatures of the wood or night spirits troubling the house, and the knowledge of his sleeping bothered him, three nights now. Before the smell of ink reached him, permeating his brain and making him unable to breathe, he wanted to know why he was sleeping. Certainly Cristina's words were resounding, but what upset him most was why. What was it that left him unwilling to swim? Surely he had not forgotten the urgency which had carried him across the lake, instant, unseen, the same carrion sense he had gasped on the return journey, leaning at the front of the ferry with strained, incomplete breaths pulsing, shivering? Cristina then, and Cristina now, her strangling beauty, love like currency or language, and yet he did not feel like swimming for her.

He waited for the lights to change so that he could cross the road and wondered whether it was Richard, his arrival and his presence spiralled into their world. Richard was consuming, was meant to be. By design he designed their attention. But his trips and traumas were part of their whole, even his snipped tongue, his delicacy of speech. Learning and teaching were movements for Luc and Cristina together. He could not consider any seconds of Richard to be lost, valueless. Green to red, walk. He moved within sight of the print works knowing as hard as he could that Richard was not causing him to sleep. So if not Cristina and not Richard he was left only with himself, the potential influx of comfort and security, Richard's font, but he was spared the desolation of such thoughts by the acid taints of ink swirling loosely in the air. He pulled open the side door of the works, seeping toxins, and went inside.

Cristina is anticipating an email from Namibia, where a reserve has asked her if they can use the font on the menus at the lodges. She likes animals, especially those fleet-footed herds of oryx and springbok she sees split by cats on nature documentaries. She has asked for written confirmation that the font will be used only in the lodges themselves, not in marketing or reporting documents, sits silently in front of the computer in the office at home and waits.

In Cavaglià she had learned to love quiet. Not that her father demanded it, but more that she had followed her mother's descent into silence, a void for creativity to take place. When her father was working on new ways of curving letters or refining pixellated designs of capitals the house would fall to a respectful reverie, time hanging like a siesta in his concentration, speech and footsteps impossible luxuries. For a while her older brother tried to force sounds, caused deliberate crashes to the quiet which demanded words of reproach or admonition, but after five months, when none had come, he threw himself to the honour of his mother and left home.

The quiet returned easily, gracefully, became the natural state of being. Cristina bore it with her. She hopes the email will be in English. She can recognise tongues and languages in others but speaks only Italian, French and English, the compulsory texts of her school. If the email is in English she will give her consent to the reserve, or Richard's, for that is how she makes her decisions, the benefit of her family, a subject she likes, a language.

Her shape is in Jean-Luc's head, slivers of her black hair across her forehead mixing with the peculiar, violet smell of shades of yellow ink. He thinks perhaps he might have disregarded her too carelessly, that he was too quick to believe his passion for her has not changed. Methyl fumes make it hard to concentrate. He does not need to work, could rest at home with Richard and survive in the hazy profits of the font. Richard is at school. It is hard to concentrate. "Would I swim to her?" he asks, and gloss paper disappears in front of him, the latest insert for the free papers, this week's offers, coupon valid from the twelfth to the nineteenth only.

The roller wash gave him headaches when he first started. He is used to the chemical fumes now, all except white ink, the rare expensive prints onto coloured paper. Soon he will sit in the front office and order the next run, define and highlight the job requirements on the screen, check for compatibility. Her shape lingers, Italian, prone to passivity. He loves her as before, personally, knowingly, a small closing of her left eye when she is indecisive, the spread of her toes to relax, a wish, a smile, the capture of her eyes. He will swim for her. The yellow inks smell of violets and acid, sounds like the rapid threats of pulsing blood from the blades cutting to the required size, trim, fold. They will swim this weekend, all of them, Richard too. It is not Cristina. He watches the paper disappear and hopes for sleeplessness.

Maman Sulpice is worse, lies in the spools of her pillows and fails to hear the wind. The blind at her window has been pulled up and its cords tied away for the winter. Her curtains are open, will remain pointlessly apart until a nurse closes them again in the evening. It is Sunday, and Maman Sulpice can barely see the lights above her head now. The sense of light advancing and receding through the window beside her has gone. She keeps her hand cupped to her ear while Fabrice is there, will not give away how much her arm aches until he has gone.

"No flowers today, Doudou? I can still use my nose."

"It's Sunday. I didn't want to bring you supermarket flowers. It doesn't seem right."

She uses her hand to push her head into a nod, smiles grimly. "Thank you." Her shoulders have sunk into their supports. Clean, white linen lies under a pillow from home, pale blue and edged with lace. A nurse said she shouldn't have it, that it could block her nose if she turned her head at night, but she insisted, 'a remembrance of who I am', and refuses to let its case be washed. Below her shoulders her chest has squashed towards her waist, and a small pain in her spine is nursing her constantly, reminding her of her purpose.

"What do you look like, Doudou?"

Fabrice laughs, partly sincerely, mostly to let her know that he has sat down to her right, with his back to the blank window. "The same as I did yesterday. It wasn't that long ago."

"Don't make fun of me," she says sternly. Her voice gathers pace, accentuating her seniority.

"You know what I look like, Maman Sulpice. You see me every day, almost."

She relaxes the fingers by her ear. "You are trying to be kind, and I thank you for it, but it's not nice for someone so young." She pushes ruffled hair above her ear, softens her image. "You must realise I haven't seen you properly for a very long time now. Please, I'd like to know. Is your hair still short? Your eyes, are they clear and light? Do you look after your mouth? Tell me."

Fabrice grabs at his hair. "Yes, my hair's quite short," he replies, teasing it out between his fingers and thumb. He wonders how long is short, how clear his eyes have to be in order to qualify as light. When he was young Maman Sulpice was the one who adored his hair, would rest her hands on his cheeks and flick her fingers out to make the thick flails at his neck move. He remembers how he hated that at the time, how it made him feel self-conscious, like he was being watched and judged simply because his hair was long. Emily loved his hair long, would sit astride him and grab at the waves at the back of his head, back in the warm Toronto evenings, when his appearance was dwelt upon. Even then he was scared by her nakedness, the way she clung to her skin as though she was clearing their communication of anything which could be misconstrued.

She was beautiful, more so to Fabrice when she strolled away from the bedroom to the bathroom or kitchen, her back swaying through her flat, her shoulders and arms engaged in the next activity, almost remote. Through the winter of ice barricading the door to the small, city garden he warmed himself next to her, and she to him, pleading with him not to be so serious and intending. As soon as they got in from the day's shops and cafés or the night bars she would begin to undress, slowly losing layers as the flat warmed. Yet it was not enticing, insinuating flesh she revealed but her own comfort, naked and uninhibited.

Fabrice looked away, drew claims of protest and shame. He could not tell her that it was her smile he was avoiding, the hot confidence of her mouth, a meaning he took from the particular fit of her teeth and the centre points of her top lip. In her smile he saw that Lake Ontario was not Lake Geneva. The tall, thin buildings of six or seven flats were not the same as the old apartment buildings in Evian, no matter how much he and Emily might each want them to be. Toronto has orange cabs, he remembers that.

"You have not told me about your mouth," Maman Sulpice insists. "Are you hiding something from me?"

"No, there's nothing to hide. I am who I have always been. Here," Fabrice says, uncurling her hand from her ear and tracing the outline of his lips with her fingertips.

It is Sunday. Lucy has showered before six, watched her face appear as the steam cleared from the bathroom mirror. She meets Alain at the cinema, safely, walks with him up into the town. The skin on his face is whitening in the cold. At the meeting point of the three restaurants they scan the menus, looking for something to say.

"Why did you leave Geneva?" Lucie asks.

"There was no one to talk to. I wanted less space around me, I suppose."

Her hair flaps across her eyes more than it did at the quayside, waiting for the boat. It is longer now, looser. "Sometimes I like parts of the city. I go there to be on my own." She turns to a different menu to stay away from the airport, the starred mornings, light inside as synthetic as the walls or the static departures board, 07.15, on time.

"I don't like being on my own. It wears me." Alain rereads the familiar list in front of him, seafood and pasta, beef, Italian chicken. Marie, and her signature, 'love, Marie', the clouds in the whites of her eyes each day when she got home from teaching, her fascination with his skin, the curve of his elbows, his forearms, when he was still looking at her, not watching.

30

"Which one would you like to go in?" he asks, seafood and pasta, four choices of salad, desserts.

"Maybe it's the silence."

In the night airport, even on the drive there as the roads begin to quiet around her, thinning, widening, the background noise is more noticeable. Electrical cables throb. Lights ache against the darkness around them, the rumour of nothing. Wheels on cleaning trolleys and cars loop whispers. Essential machines of the city's reasoning sing roundels. And in their magic, in a bass line beneath it, you can hear the quiet tumbling to be noticed. These are the words which entice Lucy, an incessant murmur for those who listen, understand, who can make out the presence of language by its absence. The sound too which was left to Alain and drove him to the rambling hush of Evian, to where he can talk, be able to look at nothing. From one of the restaurants come only the clanks and scrapes of dinner, from the others standard songs and melodies, music to be unheard and ignored in conversations at tables. Shutters above clash shut for the night. If you listen closely you can hear each wooden slat ringing out, distinguishable.

"You can't hear the quiet," Lucie says, joining him at the menu board and secretly slipping her arm in his, the cold, the music. "You can't talk in Geneva because you don't know if anybody can hear you."

"And you? Did you mind me talking to you at the cinema, and at the café before that?"

"I'm here. I can hear you." She squeezes her arm lightly into his wrist. "This one? My brother says the lamb is wonderful."

Alain thinks of bread and tomatoes, yoghurt, water, and leads her to the music. Manes is taking his last breaths as work starts. The mist in Geneva is different, does not bring him sensations of the hanging dawns on the steppes of Darjeeling, not even memories. A man and a woman walk past him, their blue coats and travel cases swishing behind them. They say nothing, do not smile. The need comes to him to call goodnight, but the quiet is not quiet.

5
Cavaglià

Cristina has always wanted the kitchen she has now. At one end of the space are maple cabinets, traditionally plain and severe, among which she has affirmed simple, coded messages of her place and identity. The handles on the cabinets are each different, some wood, some metal, some porcelain, two expensive, glass idiosyncrasies from Venice. The counters are made of granite and marble, slices cut into and around each other, speckled grey and streaked cream resting, here to cut, to chop, here to prepare, ingredients neatly arranged, here to leave to wipe and wash. She has included a few extravagances from Richard's font, the finest cooker and stylish silver or black appliances, a knife block with blades her mother had heard about in Cavaglià, knives which could slice as neatly and silently as words.

It is Cristina's kitchen. The workspace is not efficient or ergonomic. The cooking triangle is uneven, scalene, a walk to carry from the fridge to the granite, a stretch to the sink and back. She has room, a table she does not need, an extractor fan whose whirrs and drones interrupt her thinking. There is nowhere to keep a tea towel. But it is definably hers, a proclamation.

At the far end, away from the cabinets and their haphazard handles, is a second, smaller table for Richard, and past that are two doors. The left leads to the dining room, on through to the lounge. Cristina is visible through the other door. She is sitting in her office, a hidden shelter, facing the screen, waiting quietly for typed interest from Bratislava. For seven months she has read their discussions, the proposals and counter-proposals, has been promised a decision before Christmas. Before she would have worried, mingled her scents into Luc's ink when he returned from work, challenging him, anxiety edging onto her lips as she kissed him home. But she has sold permission to a search engine, and she, or rather Richard, will receive nineteen thousandths of a cent each time a page is displayed in his font. If the engine's predictions are correct they will be rich, a quarterly transfer through their accountant, and the interest related from Bratislava or the industrial conglomerate in Frankfurt are now merely distractions, quiet, happy diversions for the clouded hours while Richard is at school.

Cristina's back is straight, her legs curled up and under the chair for support. She clicks through a last check of her mail programs and disconnects. Her long, shaded hair is shielding most of her long, latin neck, slow falls waving to her shoulders. Behind her Richard sees the falls twitch in that familiar way, her expression of conclusion, knows she will be able to hear him now if he talks to her.

"Why do the trees have so much to say in the wind?" He is sitting at the table, his table, picking slices of cheese from an after-school sandwich lunch. The emmental is fresh and expensive, hangs from his fingers without tearing.

The computer sounds its farewell chimes and Cristina swivels in her chair. "They have nothing to say. They're only moving in the wind."

"They make noises," Richard protests.

"No they don't. The wind makes the noises." She walks to the table, sits down across the corner from him and drinks from his bottle of water. "Think about what causes them, the movement."

Richard slowly waves the slice of cheese hanging from his fingers. He pulls it closer, leans his tilted head to the motion.

"I can't hear anything. Mama, listen," he says, the last word coming more like 'histen', a stubborn, slow-receding interference from his snipped tongue.

She smiles at his misunderstanding, even at his 'histen'. Love, and its reflections. The oak beneath her arms is fragmented, reflects its use and history. She thinks for a moment how it would have creaked as a tree, slow, young sways while it found its strength. The grain is marked with water rings from childhood glasses, dents and scratches of Richard's play, impressions of its purpose.

Across from her is Richard's schoolbag. She pulls it towards her and unzips it, removes the empty snack box and his jumper. An envelope is curled into the bottom of the bag, where it has rested for at least two days.

The school will close for Christmas on December 20th, and reopens on January 4th.

We would like to remind you that the children will be presenting their play, 'A Christmas Wish', on December 19th at 14.00. All family members are welcome to come to watch the performance, written by the children themselves. There will be a drink and snack party afterwards.

Happy Christmas from all the staff, and we hope a prosperous New Year comes to you.

Cristina reads the letter twice to confirm her reading. She is worried about the school and Richard, see the failures of grammar in an alien language, 'will close' and 'reopens', the implication that the party will have only one snack and drink, the hope that 'New Year comes to you'. Yet it seemed to be such a good school, the best in the town, and Richard was learning to speak and write fluently in spite of his afflictions with the letter L. She hopes the letter is an aberration, written by an administrator charged with the action, worries nevertheless that they should be able to communicate effectively.

She smoothes out the sheet's folds and holds it up close to Richard, with the print facing her. "Blow this."

He blows obediently. The letter waves smoothly away from him. "Blow harder."

Again he does as he is told, makes the paper bend violently towards his mother's face. The letter refuses to speak. She turns in her chair, shifts her legs out from under the oak tree and aims herself directly at him. With a deep, silently drawn breath she blows the paper in her hand, and it crackles away and into itself like a wood fire.

She smiles at the rustling and Richard. "Did you hear that? I blew hard on it, like a wind, and the force of my breath made it bend and creak. Did you hear it?"

"Yes," Richard says. He curls the whole slice of cheese into his mouth, as if to muffle his approaching words. "The letter rustled. The paper made sounds."

"And the trees," she replies, missing his interpretation, "when the wind is strong enough, it moves them too."

"And they make sounds. I told you, Mama, the trees speak."

"But only because the wind is moving them."

"They're still making noise," Richard says, chewed slivers of emmental hiding the 'stih' of 'still'. He takes his jumper from the table and rubs its scents of home across his cheek. "Can I go upstairs?"

Cristina looks at his empty plate, sees him pick up the bottle of water, and nods. She watches him put the jumper on top of his head, the smell balancing carefully as he leaves her. She scratches at the oak with her fingernail, hears only the sound of herself.

Jean-Luc has a headache when she rings him. He is sitting in front of the folding machine, leans every one and three-quarter minutes to lift a hundred more take-away menus into a box, two thousand three hundred to go. The yellow ink smells like violets.

After she calls he leaves early, drives home in daylight. Richard is upstairs. At the same table she tells him about their conversation, his apparent fears, cheese to hide the letter L and misgivings.

"It's almost Christmas," she says, hinting to decisions about their onrushing wealth.

"Tomorrow," Jean replies, "instead of work."

He has made them both coffee, drinks his to quell the violet headache squalling at his eyes. He sips slowly, consistently, lets aspirin seek out his retinas. She would ask him what he means, tomorrow, but he has relapsed into the release of chemicals. The sound of an aeroplane comes from upstairs, moves with footsteps from the bedroom and descends to the kitchen.

"You're early," Richard exclaims, and hugs his father, turning in the middle of his hug to kiss the hair smothering Cristina's cheek, an act of forgiveness.

She bends to the kiss, lingers leaning in its glow. She could try to talk to Luc again later, wonders while he chatters to Richard about nothing where his words have gone. For he has taken to her silence, the sweet quiet she brought with her from Italy, the pure, sated sound at the edges of ski runs, where the snow is hard packed ice. There are stains of lucidity on those edges, the same view Lucy searches for in the newspapers, a corrosion sneaking around Fabrice in the Manitoba clearings. And Jean-Luc too, he rests in the evenings when Richard is asleep, smells the rumours of quiet from Cavaglià.

She could try to talk to him, yes. But she has saturated the house and their language, lives in passivity because she cannot be heard. She waits for Richard and Jean-Luc to end their rattling chatter, tries not to hear her son's use of H where he should say L. What, then, 'instead of work'? If she moves away from the table Jean will talk to her, ask her where she is going or if there is anything she would like him to do. Richard's head will lift from his father's chest to watch her. If she stays in her chair they will continue to talk, what happened at school, their respective lunches, a plan of play or Luc's stories, intricate and warm. They will not notice her silence because she is silent. The afternoon spins away with Jean-Luc's headache and Richard, fabled, fabulous hours. How can she be heard? Cristina is happy to watch them pass, waits contentedly with the view of her husband and son for another time, another passage of speech.

Tomorrow comes, carries a whisper of snow as far down as the town. Lucy walks to the straight stretch of road above the hospital, feels passionate burns of acid in her thighs as she climbs the loops and curls. She realises it has been months since she walked in the hills, hears the cold calling her back to them before the sloped tarmac on the route is too icy, before the spikes in the verge are waving orange tape to mark the boundaries. She is wearing her old boots, a stale, stable pair she bought in a sale three years ago, this weekend only, final reductions. As she walks they are starting to bend again, flexion in the ankle protection, a loosening of their summer wardrobe black stiffness. She nears the straighter run of road, sees the dark grey cast by the trees in the light grey. Her boots begin to understand her language of walking, and are easy.

The ditch to her left, the downward side, is filled with the mulch of leaves, sweating to themselves. She can smell their hunger, the act of rotting, of generating heat as the weeks cool to winter. The bottom of the ditch is wet with their sweat, water from the hanging air. Firs hold out their hands to keep their portion of the sky in place. She thinks of Brel as she slows, *Vesoul*. Alain doesn't like Brel. He heard *Mathilde* from an apartment across from hers when she cooked him dinner, asked if he could close the balcony doors to shut him out. She said yes, didn't tell him how the fever of the singing made her blush.

"Fool," he said. "How could anyone be that excited about Mathilde coming back?"

"It's just a romantic song. He loves her."

"Then why did he let her leave?" Alain smiled at the confusion. "I know it's only an expression of passion, and that's good."

"The expression?"

"The passion. And yes, the declaration of it too, but if he's that passionate then why didn't he go after her, instead of staying at home with his mother and his maids?"

Lucie flipped the plastic top from a bottle of wine, red to match the blood of the meat and her new, scarlet tablecloth, bought for the occasion, his first dinner. "We don't know why, he doesn't tell us. Perhaps he couldn't go, perhaps she went with her family. But his excitement, can't you feel it?"

"No. Yes." He closed the doors and the sound was gone. Wine splashed noisily into two glasses. "It's old-fashioned."

"It's romantic."

"No it isn't, it's unrealistic. It would have been more romantic if he'd gone after her." Geneva, Marie. He could have gone after her but there was no romance to chase.

Lucy sings Brel to herself on the road, *Vesoul* as a car drives past her, too fast, too close. Alain kissed her at the door that night, a gentle, fragile movement of his head when they said goodbye. She remembers how quickly he turned his eyes away afterwards, how she worried then that he was only being polite, doing what was expected of him. Three weeks and four cooked meals later he stayed for the first time, at her tender request.

Another car crashes by. Its headlights are on even though it is eleven o'clock in the morning. The light between the trees has its own colour, shades which are brighter than dark but less energetic, as if the woods on either side are soaking away the brilliance in return for protecting the town from avalanches. Another car, silver, lights on full beam reflecting in her eyes. She wishes the full snow would hurry up, to slow the traffic.

The road curves and slopes. She is walking downhill, comfortable in her boots and the moments of quiet while the trees ache. Ahead of her and across she sees an orange movement, fast and irregular, stopping, starting, stopping, familiar. She recognises Jean-Luc and Cristina picking angles through the beech and pine twenty metres into the wood. The orange movement disappears and reappears, flitting in and out of her sight like Morse code. She cannot decide on his signals, come here and join us or leave us alone, keep to your damp, cerebral road and let us play. A hunger comes to her. Food, urgent and plain, something mechanical and fulfilling like bread or fruit, an action for her jaw, as if the sensations of taste have scurried to reclaim her from the scents of the ditch and the hanging air. They will drag her back to connectivity, those tastes, give her substance on which to hold.

Yet before that rescue in the simplicity of her apartment she must say hello to her nephew, in case they have seen her. She crosses the road to the dangerous side, where the cars will not notice her until they pass. The Braille of trees makes it harder for her to see through. Her perspective is shortened. Cristina is in the open. Jean-Luc's voice is carolling beneath the branches but Lucy cannot hear what he is saying.

"Which one, Richard? Pick one. A tall, big one." Luc has brought them to listen. He tried to lead them past the top of their garden but Richard would not go there, not to the night woods, not even in the milky, winter daylight. He had clung to his mother's legs, hidden, forced a sob to emphasise his resistance.

"What about this fir?" Jean-Luc asks. "It's very strong. Look how tall it is, and how wide it is down here."

"The house," Cristina says.

Richard runs back to his father's voice. The orange coat is still too big for him and its thick padding makes his arms stick out sideways like young, mobile branches. "It's too big. It will make a loud noise."

"Not without the wind, and there isn't any. Can you feel the wind in here? Can you hear it making any leaves rustle, up there?" Jean-Luc squats down, lets the side of his head touch Richard's. He points upwards. "Listen."

"No, I can't hear this one. It doesn't want to talk to us."

Cristina is before them, beside the tree. She too leans slightly to the bark, almost expecting to hear the sap breathing. She watches Luc and Richard, her need, her expression. Their faces are hers, and their words. "I think it's a good idea, Jean. But the house," she insists.

"There's no sound coming because there's no wind." Jean-Luc's voice vibrates on Richard's temple, a vivid hum through his skull.

"Perhaps this tree has nothing to say now. But in the night the noise is louder."

"It only seems louder because there is less other noise to get in the way."

Richard considers this, lifts his head free to listen for sounds.

"And there is no wind, so these woods are quiet now," Luc says, pressing his explanations into Richard's silence. "The wind makes the trees move, and the wood creaks sometimes. Think how logs crackle and snap in the fire. They are made from trees. If you step on a twig it cracks when it breaks." He looks around for a stick, big enough to hear, dry enough to break, sees Cristina smiling over them and the tea green of the bark against the black of her hair, a comfort, a desire. For an instant he wishes Richard was not with them, wants to pull her down and slide her free curls against damp leaves, or dive into the lake with her and hold her close, watching the sunlight refracting on her naked shoulders.

He finds a fallen branch near her leg. It is thin and beginning to decay, and as he reaches out to take it he brushes his hand against her ankle. She twitches. He rubs the inside of her calf and squeezes it, more than affectionately, then takes hold of the branch and withdraws, happy in the passion she has shown to his idea. He has a plan for the house, believes it won't cause them concern.

Behind their low forms Cristina recognises Lucy stepping carefully across the ditch by the road. Her coat is brown and undone, catches on the few brambles able to survive in the light of the road. Lucy's black boot slips on mud under leaves and she has to tilt her body forward to catch her balance. She is more used to resistance, Cristina thinks, or snow.

38

"I'll make this bend and break," Jean says to Richard. "You'll hear sound, and it will be me making it happen."

Lucy is behind them, stops to let the action take place in precious quiet. A car goes past on the road, thirty metres away. Its engine note and wheel rumbles fade, like light.

"Alain must be good for you," Cristina says. "You would have fallen before, when you slipped."

The branch cracks cleanly. Its crack has no echo, not in the winter when there is less growth on which to rebound. Richard's eyes are startled wider, in spite of his expectation.

"You made a loud noise."

"Yes, I did." Jean-Luc drops the broken pieces of branch and hugs Richard, one arm wrapped around his ribs so that their cheeks are touching.

Richard squeezes back in excitement, hoping to generate a moment for him to be spun around. When no spinning follows he pulls an arm free and picks up one half of the branch, holds the dry, white end out to Cristina. "Papa made a loud noise, didn't he?" he says, then swivels back to his hug, the snapped end waving around dangerously.

"Yes, I did," repeats Jean-Luc. "And at night the wind makes the noises, not the trees."

Richard does not hear him. He has twirled so far around that he has seen Lucy, and points the splinters at her. "Oose."

Luc looks up at Cristina's eyes, watching Lucy. He sees her recognition, beyond that a frame in the brown-grey light of his wife and her small, needing clamours. He senses the need to hold her again, this time not in passion but with the claim of what he calls love, to keep her in a warm, safe embrace, be near the smell of her, a want just to feel her body breathing, the swell, the fall, her mouth and those dark wood eyes resting happily, where they choose.

Without turning away from her face or letting go of Richard he calls out to his sister, standing still in the silence behind him. "Luce, we're going to spend some of the font money."

"Oose," shouts Richard.

6
Toronto

Fabrice stopped in Toronto only for the shortest of recollections on his way back from the study cabins of Manitoba. He wanted to be alone, left quickly for the airport and the desertion of five hours until his flight, away from the intimations of Emily and her naked affection. She had said as much as she could, held back the coercion of love and all its accompanying stresses, the lowering of her gaze, a shine of the curves of skin on her upper arms. Instead she made them both tea as he unpacked his things from the trip and repacked his bags for Evian.

"So how did the research go? Did you find what you wanted?"

"Perhaps."

"And now it's back to France, to write up all the work."

"Yes."

She was standing by the sink, trying not to rest nonchalantly while he gathered the possessions he had left with her. It would be unfair to sit, she thought. Too much like abandonment. They had not declared anything, made promises or imagined together what might happen afterwards. But that's not to say that it was casual, a coupling merely for a season, convenience, opportunity. No, their courtship had been natural, fulfilling, and it was only as he sought out the few missing clothes that she realised the finality of his weeks in the national park.

"Your good trousers are in the wardrobe. I washed them."

"Thanks."

"On the right, second shelf from the bottom."

"Thanks," Fabrice repeated. She was fully dressed. Their conversation was more than polite. It frightened him that they could be so courteous and unconnected when they had been intricate, unprotecting. Perhaps it was the lack of self-preservation before, or more the lack of need for self-preservation. The longed-for summer would arrive soon enough. Fabrice knew that her face would not be the same when he next saw it, if he ever did.

"What was it like, at Riding Mountain?"

He had found his good trousers, folded neatly beneath two pairs of hers which she had worn while he was away. He took hold of hers, lifted them gently to slide his out. He didn't know what to say, how to describe the trees and their moods.

"The cabins were better than I thought they would be."

Later, at the airport, he remembered that phrase and wondered how he had come to choose it. She had asked about the park and he had answered with the cabins. Why? And why, after her tea-stained silence, had he then gone on to talk about Jean-Christophe and the welcome conversation in French, about Kennet looking for Scandinavian forests in other countries, about Max and Diane? He kept their proclamations about the trees to himself, of course. He had not had an affair with the forest, in spite of Diane's knowing, reflexive insistence, 'she's like a lover'. No, that was not him. He was not romantic about the basics of regeneration and decay. But he told Emily how Max and Diane used to intertwine their little fingers as they ate. That, and the cabins.

"It's probably the only physical contact they ever have," she said, a flash of her eyes slipping some of her clothing from her shoulder, an intimation of herself, their past.

He had almost finished packing, drew his trousers out from under hers. This is what it feels like to pull apart, he thought, to slide out and away. The cotton of his good trousers moved easily across the thicker, heavier blend of hers.

"Do we have time to eat?" She spoke lightly, feeling the brutality of the apartment.

"No."

"What time's your flight?"

"Twenty past two," he lied. "I'd better get going. You know what the traffic is like before lunch."

At the airport he found his check-in desk and wandered around the terminal. A large, roof-high area at one end of the building was shielded by long, flat sheets of whitewashed wood, with unmarked sheets of opaque plastic fixed to the screen as some kind of intermittent decoration or deterrent. Fabrice walked past the not-signs, wound an arc along the edge of the great, hidden chamber. Eventually he went outside, to the cold drizzle and mist so unlike that of the forest, and rested his forehead against the tinted glass to peer through.

The secret, private room was blank. Stray cables curled in loops from gaps in the ceiling. Dust and lethargy lay on the floor like winter light settled on Evian. He thought of home and of Emily. To his left, in the deep of the chamber, a second, interior wall of wood was spread across the entrance to the temporary world of the departure lounge, No Entry and No Exit signs straddling the doorless opening in two languages. For a reason he could not explain he noticed the

French first, saw it caverning out at him even though all the signs in the airport were bilingual.

Emily. Accès Interdite and Sans Issue. He took the magnetic monorail to Terminal Three, found a snack bar in which to waste time and the last of his dollars.

Lucy will help, as Lucy does. At the water's edge she is avoiding talking to Fabrice's predecessor in the cinema hours. Jacques is nineteen and annoying, nothing like that other Jacques with his foul, rampaging teeth and impassioned sweat. She has seen the black and white footage of Brel, the cunning shadows and light to make him historical, a myth. On the stage beneath him the penumbral circles vibrate when he kicks out to emphasise. Hear me, his characters plead. Listen to what I have to say. This is life, my death, and yours.

The lake breathes back to her. This Jacques, in full glorious colour, is nothing like life. Once he tried to touch her, rubbed his hand on her back and let his arm fall over her shoulder. She pulled swiftly to her right, twisting away, knowing that it was only arrogance or youth, an imagined cinematic camaraderie perhaps. Since then he has held himself to speech. When the auditorium doors have closed and the audience is securely in its seats he follows her outside, 'a full room' or 'I thought there would have been more for this' leading him towards her. When Lucy was young she fished for crabs with pieces of chicken skin, piled them up into her bucket. Jacques keeps his space away from her, late trickling sun and the sounds of Evian behind her, waking. She lets him speak to her, turns and nods politeness, a random smile if he happens to continue, but he loses force without her replies, drags and drifts into nothingness as the daily chatter dies.

She can see across the lake, a swimmer's destination, can turn to her left or right to the headlands pushing out, sequences of eager spills. On some there are trees, natural expansions of woodland on land fallen from the mountains. On others there are villas with private quays, swings for children, a place to park and watch the light fall on the water, as Lucy does now.

Yes, she will help. The silence comforts her. Jacques will take the delicate values of his nineteen years and set them to work in a restaurant, charming tips from the tourists and contacts from the residents. He will lead six girls into his bedroom that summer, enthuse them in a resemblance of passion. Three times a girl will leave with disappointment. The other three times he will wake and wonder why he finds himself in the empty spaces of his chest, behind his breathing.

When Jacques departs for the restaurant and a social whirl Fabrice will take the job at the cinema to fill the quiet of his return, though he does not yet know it. At the water Lucy will help. In Terminal Three he chewed slowly on the oversized slice of pizza his dollars had offered him, a reheated performance of a regular incident. The slices of tomato were oily and yet still dry. The cheese was tough, pre-cooked and stale. It made him think of young days with Lucien, whose family owned an Italian restaurant and refused to use anything other than the finest Neapolitan mozzarella. Lucien and he would be given the delicacy of cold pizza, on which the mozzarella was always congealed into sinewy, organic pools. The Canadian offering was worse. Tepid strings of hydrogenated vegetable fat pretended to be hot, fresh cheese. He thought of France and her customs, the wondrous range and styles of cheeses, innate definitions of the beauty of the hills and herds, wide green fields leading to a single milkman and cheesemaker in his kitchen and cellar, prime, raw curd, infected with young old bacilli, naked.

Emily, naked under the lips of her clothes. From a souvenir shop on the concourse he heard the clear lifts of an Irish accent, the sound instantly recognisable from the Toronto lakefront and the bars near Liberté. South of Dublin, Fabrice thought. Perhaps even as far down as Carlow. He pulled another slice from the plate, gazed down at the oils and yellow laces, and lost his appetite. The food had only been a diversion to kick away the hours. Three more until he left her.

The airport was cold. Air purifiers cleansed and cycled, pumped brisk, chilled gasps into the terminals. Fabrice saw the hairs on his wrist standing up in the brittle air, looked from his watch to the ceiling vents and the spare breaths urging towards him. He stood up to walk to the Irish voice, a passage of time. Its female owner was selling towels with pictures of seals and huskies to two elderly tourists, who were clumsily shifting and swapping their bags to free a hand for a wallet.

"Guaranteed quality, they are, and there's an address here on the label if you have a problem, which I know you won't. There you go, would you like a bag? What brings you to Canada then? A holiday, I'll guess, I've never been to the Far East myself, but I'd like to, sorry, your passport, Cambodia." She was older than her voice. Her greying hair and black, magpie eyes made Fabrice think of the seals on the towels, as if one of them had hidden themselves away in the capitalist world and was secreting funds back to the rest of the herd, corruption from within. He could not understand how she had chosen to represent herself as Irish, but the deceit was working.

The tourists were led to matching bathrobes, "As clean and pure as the Yukon snow." Their purchases grew. They were swept by her cadences, caught by their lack of her language and the swift, including smiles of her words. Carlow, he thought, almost certainly.

"Excuse me," he said, when the Cambodian couple had retreated, beaten and happy. "Have you lived in Toronto for a long time?"

She stole shy magpie glimpses at his shoes and watch, at the strap of his rucksack broken by a cut branch in Manitoba. "About fourteen years now. My husband moved us here when they closed the plant back home, rest his soul. Why do you ask, now?" She stressed the H in why, aspirating it unnecessarily, Ireland, her husband, an unexpected remembrance, welcome and warm.

"You've kept your accent," he said, adding "I have friends in Casteldermot," to elicit confirmation.

"Castledermot. Near Carlow? I think one of my cousins moved near there, but I've so many it's hard to keep track. I've never been myself."

"No?"

"No. Before we moved here I hadn't been anywhere. There was the odd trip into Dublin, for shopping and all, and we used to visit my grandparents in Antrim before the borders became, you know, awkward. But apart from that I just stayed in Finglas. I grew up there, I met my husband there, and I lived there with him until he was relocated over here. Do you know Finglas? Of course it's part of north Dublin now, but back then it was a town all by itself."

Fabrice looked behind her, saw the precious tourist images of Canada, wolves, polar and brown bears, beavers, the mounted police statuettes, a small case containing hand-made jewellery depicting totems and inukshuks, delicate silver Canadian geese in flight. To his left he saw the maple leaf on every white or red sweater, rows of caps and shirts, above them boxes of chocolates, jars of syrup. But those keepsakes were of another Canada, not the one which Max and Diane knew, where the trees fell in love and the cabins hummed with anticipation and desire. And it was not Emily's Canada, skin in the light from the bathroom window, open sandwiches of cheese and ham in front of the television or under the sounds from her radio, in bed, warm and untroubled, nor was it the black and orange cabs with their sting as they zipped through the cold night streets to another evening at the waterfront.

He longed instantly to be clear of the airport, to be free at 38,000 feet heading back to the stiller waters at Evian. Canada was not his country, not anymore. It was as foreign to him as Finglas was to the

44

accent before him, still swaying to its own rhythm, twitching here and there about the stone house and the luxury now, in spite of her husband's death, God rest his soul.

"I have to catch my flight."

"Of course you do. Listen to me here, going on and on. Have a good trip now, won't you? Are you sure you wouldn't like a book or something, to remember the place by? I can see you haven't been here on holiday, but from the look in your eye I'd say you weren't coming back in a hurry. A shame, though, because it's a marvellous land."

In the café Astrid is preparing for summer. She turns off the tall freezer and empties it of its winter supplies, throws away most of the cakes, the light cheesecakes and pastry concoctions, places the dark chocolate entities in the coldest fridge while ice drips from the freezer's shelves. April, and the snow has begun to seep into the hillsides. The trade changes. Weekends only, until the holiday season and the migration to the deep lined green.

"What will you do now?" Lucy asks. She is leaning, trying not to make Astrid aware of her height. Behind her two small families have been prising the last from the slopes while they can, children collected from school in the expanding afternoon light to be rushed to the high lifts, where the snow persists. They are talking loudly. The radio is off and the younger voices ricochet around the still, wood chamber.

"Now? I've just got to adjust the till for the new prices and clean out the pastry display, then we can sit down and talk, if that's what you want."

"But this is closing now."

Astrid looks at the clock on the far wall, white face, black streaks. "It's only three. There's an hour to go yet."

It is raining, a wide, persistent spring rain pushing the low snow deep into the ground. The windows of the café are smeared with condensation and a faint heat. Ice cracks loose in the freezer. It echoes as it lands, bounces fragments through the open door onto the newspaper below. Astrid turns at the sound, sees the dark grey damp widening. Lucy sees the business pages, revenue, competition, combustion.

Astrid makes them both fresh coffee and sits at the table nearest the counter, an easy escape for her should another customer arrive. The snow is washing through the grass.

"What shall I do until the summer, Lucy? I have to do something. The weekend isn't enough to keep me going."

"I don't know."

"April. Everything changes, just when I get settled into it."

Lucy listens for more ice falls but the children are too loud. Drips cannon like the repeating of a heartbeat, hollow and insistent. Perhaps you imagine that she is hearing the silence between them, the emptinesses, there in that wooden building wedged between the top of the road and the bottom of the slopes. Or that she is listening to the heat fading into trails of water on the windows. What led her there, to that silence, caused her to listen for a heartbeat, while rain fell on the town, waiting, watching?

In the footwell of a black Fiat a bag of freshly bought apples and lemons rolled around the corners of Geneva. Alain had chosen the apples carefully, looked attentively into the boxes to find the ones he wanted. He had often stopped at that particular corner, at the long, thin shop which refused to close in spite of the pressures of the city. There he would buy more bottles of water to replenish, fresh herbs and oils, slices of that peculiar Polish sausage. Sometimes he would walk through the alleys to the old town and gaze through the windows of the shoe shops and the bright, sparse boutiques, looking for a particular shade of apple green, the colour of passion. The lemons too were for Marie, but she has already gone.

The streets were wet, he remembers, like they seemed to have been all winter, even on the dry days of November and February, between the snows. He turned the car towards home, followed an automatic path from the active thoughts of shopping. The tyres slipped noisily on the tarmac. The news had finished and he turned off the radio to hear the road shrinking into him. A fruit rolled free of the bag, detaching itself from the company of apples and lemons. Alain heard it echo as he cornered, felt the mirror of the road at the edge of his sight and hearing. He glanced down to realise the image of the fruit, apple or lemon, cruel eyes beating into the gloom, saw the red skin against the dark charcoal carpet. The inside wheel hit the kerb and bounced the car back across the damp. The apple too, reacting to the sudden, unsuspected forces, recoiled from its demonstration and clung back to the crowd, yellow, red, vague shaping shades of green as Alain's hands slipped to instinct on the wheel. The noise of the road changed its pitch.

When Geneva is wet the city busies itself in the lustre. Business umbrellas become more than accessories of power, symbols as realised as the neon stripes denominating wealth on the office buildings. The cars and coats are another way to be heard, identifying marks which saunter through the streets, never rushing, time to spare. Newspaper kiosks and bus stops retreat into themselves, seek protection from the spray in condensed, huddled masses, yearning against the weather. On the corner of Rue de la Servette and Place de Montbrillant a vendor closed the side doors of his kiosk to protect his magazines as the rain began to fall again, a light, sweeping rain he knew from the red ski runs at the top of his favourite hill, advanced, experienced skiers only, beware of low clouds and trees.

He held his newspapers in place with three orange bricks, bright in the sun but dampened without it to rust, was known as L'Homme Rouille to the regulars who bought from him on their way to the station in the early mornings. As the apple brought another rustle from the bag he heard the complaints of tyres and looked up to see the dull crunch of metal and metal, the subdued splintering of headlights, Alain's Fiat slipping across and into the front of an oncoming car. For two hours the police inspected the impact, took details and swept the road. L'Homme Rouille had closed up his kiosk. Alain drove his damage home in semi-darkness, his one working headlight picking out half the route. He left the lemons in the car, remembered to take the two bottles of water for her from the back seat, and found her missing in the darkness, "I've failed your inspection, love, Marie."

Lucy gently relaxes herself across from Astrid, aware of her height. Between them two cups of coffee are going cold. Stains are settling into the edge of each cup, making themselves content to wait until they are called to move. At the only other table still occupied the children are eating or drinking, or simply tired, and their parents are watching to see if the rain will carry on falling. It is time to leave, perhaps, to drive home, to feed and bathe.

"There's nothing at the cinema?"

"You know I'd tell you if there was."

Astrid sighs, accepting. "Why do we have to bother with the spring? It seems such a pointless time. Why can't we just go straight from the winter to the summer?"

"You don't mean that."

The freezer creaks with cracking ice. Astrid rubs the bridge of her nose with her thumb and forefinger, closes her eyes and frowns. "You're right." She scratches at her eyebrows, at the blank, plucked section between them. "And they'll come back. They go, and then they come back. I'll talk to Guillard. He might know somebody in town who needs help for a while, a café or a shop somewhere."

47

"He might." Lucy pours a sachet of sugar into her coffee and stirs it, hears the scrape of the melting crystals in the bottom of the cup. Silence passes, precious and incandescent.

"There was a family here from Croatia last week. I don't know why. You'd think they would go to the Olympic centre at Bjelolasica, or to Sljeme. But she had the strangest jacket, the mother." Astrid looks across to the cluttered table, sees coats and hats being readied. "It was the colour of lemons, all except the sleeves and collar. They were red, and made of a different material. It made her look like she had cut two coats and stitched them into one."

"Perhaps she had."

The family stands slowly, the parents first and then the children reluctantly accepting their walk through the rain to the car park. The glass in the front door rattles as it closes behind them, streaks of condensation turning to water in the breaths of outside air.

Astrid drinks her coffee quickly, easing it into her throat in an instant motion. She moves to clear the family's table of their plates, glasses and cups, the afterthoughts of their stay, bends to pick up a spoon and a straw from the floor. As she passes by Lucy on her way to the counter she pauses, her attention still caught by thoughts of the previous week. "The sleeves were looser somehow, more fluid. I suppose it was to make it easier to turn, to bend your elbows into the corners."

Heat moves with her, strains in the circled air and the currency of progression, an empty café, minutes further to closing. More drops fall on the newspaper. In the pressure of that cabin they could be Astrid's anxious murmurs, symptoms of the closing season and the long approach to summer. Even the rain has a warmth to it, colours of growth. It falls on the path to the car park and the road away like footsteps. Lucy stirs her sugar, long dissolved. She can hear the sodden print spread out by the freezer, the beats landing on it with a regular, immutable pulse. They remind her of the clock in her apartment when she stands on the balcony, watching the washing flutter or the litter in the street below move to the patience of passing traffic, feels like the same moments before sleep when she lies listening to the radio. But they are just drops of water thawing in the freezer, cold, new water.

Fabrice took the monorail back to Terminal One, walked from the train towards the escalator down to the concourse, and heard his name. He stopped to listen to the repeat, please, Monsieur Dumont, to the information desk.

Emily. What else could it be? He had handed over his luggage at the check-in desk, was still carrying his rucksack with its broken strap. His flight was on time, according to the display screens. There was no other reason to be called but her.

Three orange cones blocked his route. Behind a red strap acting as a barrier two men were lifting the second-top step out of the motionless escalator. The scored, metal tier looked back at him, taunting him for his eagerness and floating despair. He followed the train's other passengers to the stairs, weaved impatiently through them as they paused to lift their suitcases, and re-entered the noise of the departure hall.

What could she want from him? They had parted conscientiously at the door to her flat, Emily deciding not to go with him to the street and wait with him for the cab. She held her hands behind her back, private and secure, leant to kiss him on both cheeks twice, the European way, let him hold her for a moment longer than necessary. He released her, picked up his bags and his concealed sadness and left her intimacy. Four hours later it was back, that exposed closeness, calling him to the information desk.

He kept to the edge of the hall, wanting to see her before she saw him. What would she look like? Would she be wearing the same clothes, the brown checked trousers and white shirt as before? Would she keep her usual beige jacket on or leave it in the car, knowing the temperature in the terminal would be regulated, set to relief and departure? Or had she changed into a new outfit for the occasion, a dress with which to pull him towards her? Casual jeans perhaps, and her favourite iron-blue sweater, the weathered, round-necked comfort she wore before she got home and took it off? And her face, how would she wear that? How could you share an expression in such a public situation which was by its very intention designed to be seen only by one person? But that is to assume that you are bearing such thoughts, languages to be given over to another as best you can, not held as near to you as silence when you sit side by side in the evening, enjoying the performance. Who could imagine Emily's thoughts then, while Fabrice was letting his rucksack scrape along the wall like it had once caught the branches of trees at Riding Mountain? Even if Fabrice could have heard them, would he have understood?

He saw the silver sheen of the floor and the queues at the check-in desks and security gates. Accès Interdite and Sans Issue. She was not at the information desk, at least was not clearly visible amongst the travellers. He wondered if she was watching him approach, seeing how his body coped with the news of her.

49

An airport police officer stopped him. "Are you looking for something, Sir?" He spoke in English, the choice of language determining Fabrice as not French or Francophone, other, passing.

"The information desk?" Fabrice's voice was blurred, inconclusive. He looked at the uniform and the noticeable weapon without seeing the officer's face.

"Over there, Sir. This hall is only for passengers or those assisting them. Are you travelling today?"

Fabrice nodded and turned to look in the direction of the officer's extended arm. She was still not there, was nowhere. He created a smile of thanks and apology, and walked across the constant floor to the desk.

Two ageing women were waiting to serve him, the same women who two hours earlier had directed him to the monorail and the food court in Terminal Three. They were almost identical to each other, carried the same smiles of other post-retirement workers who found the free time overwhelming. He took a breath, inconspicuous and reinforcing. They did not recognise him.

"How can I help you?" one of the women asked in English. He could not tell which.

"Monsieur Dumont. You called me."

The women looked down at their list of messages. They ran their finger down the calls for attention, seeking his name. "No, I don't think so, Sir. We had a message for a Monsieur Dumond, but he's picked it up already. Are you sure?"

7
Cavaglia II

In the first week of March Jean-Luc and Cristina left for their grand adventure. They had waited so that Richard could practise his gliding, caught between his parents' willing separation at the top of the nursery slope as they guided him down and allowed him to fall. The white was forgiving, clean and soft, not yet hardened to the sheer compression of ice. Each time Richard's skis led him to wavering Luc and Cristina turned into him, one alongside and one below, guarding him as he tumbled laughing or frustrated to the ground. In those three weeks of the new snow year he learned how to balance and sway. Later, even years later, those weeks were the ones he remembered as the time when he was freed from falling.

They went first to the private, structured quiet of Cavaglià, with a wish to thank again, to share the unforeseen rewards of Richard's font. In the cool of a Tuesday afternoon Jean entered the strained, bright world of their home for the first time. He had met her parents, of course, at the wedding and before, had travelled to Italy and shared meals with them, but never in their house. Cristina's father was younger than he had pictured, more upright. From her descriptions and definitions he had thought of him as bent over an ancient desk, small and unkempt, working in an underlit room on the carvings which brought him his subsistence. And he would be ageing, have thin or missing grey hair and round glasses like a numinous scribe. His loose fingers would clutch vaguely at the weapons of his trade, sharp-needled pens and worn, comfortable pencils, unopened letters piled beside him like shields as he leaned to his work.

It was a strained, bright world. From the road they walked through a passage between houses and out into another street. Cristina was holding Richard's hand, even though he knew where to go, remembered it from the times when he and his mother had visited his grandparents. She let him guide them to the door then turn his hand to knock loudly, twice, three times, four times. Cristina bent down to block his hand for the fifth knock.

The house was tall and narrow, wedged in the line resting against the rambled road. Its white paint made it stand out from the other houses, nestling in their pink-brown stone like so many members of an audience who had given up waiting to speak. Jean-Luc looked at the brown window frames and shutters, saw carefully inscribed patterns on the wood edges as he listened for an indication of life behind the door.

Cristina had warned him about the silence, quietly explaining the beat measures one evening after Richard had gone to sleep. "It has its own music," she told him, "sequences of language I haven't found anywhere else."

"What do you mean?" Luc answered, her halting phrases sounding awkward and uncertain. "How can silence have its own sequences?"

"I don't know, but they do. You'll see why when we get there." She had learned about the cycles of quiet, chosen her own to match her environment. While Jean-Luc was inhaling ink at work she lived in that selection, swum through the warm solitude of the office and communicated digitally. It was only when her family came home that the fluency deserted her, left her reeling in the strange colours of another house's tempo. And the flows were not hers and not Jean-Luc's but an amalgamation, naturally different from that of Cavaglià and her father's borrowed, fluid creations. But they were her choices to make, as clearly as the kitchen counter is hers, cream and grey, maple cupboards, the collection of handles.

Lucy remains at the cinema, unseen and nameless. She passes over tickets and change, is met sometimes by Alain as she steals away for a cigarette, at other times waits for Fabrice to close the doors to the auditorium and join her in the dark cold of early spring. After the last of the viewers have gone Fabrice locks them inside to store the night's takings in the office and ready the building for the next day. On Fridays and Saturdays they walk together to the night-safe, sometimes with Alain strolling as casually as he can beside Lucie, silently, his feet rapping on the paving slabs as the breeze blows over the mountains and down to the town.

They don't talk then. What can he say to her? He has nothing to say. Fabrice walks on the other side of her, shielding the canvas bag.

Richard wriggled from his mother's grip and turned his hand to knock on the door again. His knuckles slipped on the paint and grain and he lost his balance, fell forwards into the door from the weight of his arm and the motion. The report of his impact fell unheard under his cries.

From the cinema or the bank Lucy turns to her apartment or Jean-Luc's house. She had agreed to spend three nights each week in the family home, moves on those days from room to room turning lights on and off, circles heat at night and air in the mornings. If Alain is with her they walk through the town and loop up through the thin streets to the clear roads, cross over quickly in dark quiet.

He wants to talk but she is purposeful, filled with that after work energy. She pushes on in the gradient.

"Why do you walk so quickly?"

"I don't."

"Yes, you do," he says, the y and e of yes forced out in the effort of matching her stubborn pace. It is more of a grunt than a vowel, but she gleans the yes from the s and the words which follow it.

"I'm walking, that's all."

Alain falls behind her, slides to the inside of the corner three steps after her as they turn for the last straight, watches her feet fall on the dark grey. Thirty seconds pass, another twenty, time in stride. "Yes, you are, but you're walking quickly," he says, his struggled voice rebounding from the deeper greys of the trees to their left like the last murmurs of a song.

She stops. The nearest streetlight is fifteen metres ahead of them. The skin of her cheeks and around her nose would have been glowing from the exertion, if either of them could have seen in colour. Tall branches waved over their heads. A winter mist suggested snow.

"It's cold." Alain looks up, concentrates on patterns of air tempered by the sickly lamp until he can see them move. "It's going to snow soon."

Lucie's feet have swollen inside her boots. She hates wearing them to work as it makes the journey home so much more than leaving work. The roads are threatened with ice. It is a sensible decision, made regularly. She steps to the side to illuminate his face, watches the hill and the trek leave marks on him. The first etchings of a smile are breaking through her tiredness before she speaks. "Let's go home. I'm sorry."

Home. She has never called it that, not to him. Her apartment, or his, but never home. It feels warm just to say the word, even though it is Jean-Luc's home, not hers, and Alain does not spend the night there. Her smile spills breath, visible in the chilled night looming.

At dinner Jean-Luc waited patiently for cognac and coffee, his moment. They ate at a restaurant Cristina's father had chosen, a wide, spare place where everybody knew him and yet was still surprised to see him, as if he was not expected for months, a prearranged date. "Gianluca," they called him, "Il Linguatore," the maker of language. Sophia stood a respectful distance away, his wife, her mother, allowed him to glow in his recognition until she too was welcomed, kissed, her and Cristina's chairs pulled out for them in a show of grandeur. She was the curator of words, his keeper and his custodian, and Cristina was the returning bride, dark and full, a myth gone to the other side of the mountains and the border.

Luc was introduced slowly. His name and place came first, the son. With their antipasti he was called the father, two chairs to his left Richard behaving impeccably like a good grandson should, vaguely frightened in the wood sea of plastic foliage hung from every hook and angle.

By the time the first espressi arrived Jean had graduated to husband. He had said little, left a few hidden, encouraging smiles for Richard and had his arm constantly caressed by Cristina. Or he took them for caresses, but her grasps, squeezes and rubs could easily have been seen as possession. She might have been claiming him, keeping him as hers in the face of those strangers, her other family, the town and house of before. But he took them as affection, and who could blame him under Gianluca's paternal seriousness?

He had waited, unusually quiet and abstracted. The cognac was arriving. A slow, melodious calm had infected the near-empty restaurant, a suggestion, could he have heard it, of that particular essence of beating silence which Cristina had warned him about.

"Signore," he began, "I have something for you."

"You have? And please, Gianluca."

He didn't look like Jean thought he would. They had met before, and there were photographs in the bedroom and framed on the kitchen walls, but at home and in the tremor of that restaurant he was different. Where Jean had expected a stooped, reverential quiet he had found upright indifference. He was tall, taller, omnipresent. His form ruled the motion of those around him, called for attention and restraint even in his careering laughter at the dinner table. Yet Jean could see how that presence, or rather that absence, would take the world into silent contemplation when he was working. And that work was the matter in question, the creation of texts and scripts for new communications. The creation too of a legacy, whether artistic or financial.

"Cristina has worked very hard for Richard."

Gianluca leaned forward, rested his elbows on the table and interlocked his fingers, stretching his forearms flat in front of him. His cognac glass was trapped in the triangle of his arms. "Her family is important to her," he said, turning his head to look directly at Jean.

"Did you know, Signore, that she has done many deals to allow the use of Richard's font, the one which you so generously gave him?"

"No, I didn't." Gianluca looked briefly at Cristina, smiled and blinked slowly, nodding his head once in approval. "If I had thought about it, I would have known she would. But the font was a gift to my grandson. I don't think about these things afterwards."

Luc reached into the side pocket of his best jacket and took out the envelope he had been trying to keep fresh and flat since they left the house, knowing that its appearance would be the first indication of its worth. "It is a wonderful gift you have given him, Signore."

In spite of the invitation he could not call Gianluca by his name. The high, dominant forehead and short, black hair forbade it, as did his round, childlike eyes. So too the cognac glass, safely installed where it belonged under cover of his heavy chest. He was not as fat as Jean remembered yet there was enough of him, especially in the shade of the waiters and foliage, seemingly a welcomed importance.

"She has negotiated one deal in particular, one special agreement through which your font, Richard's font, will be seen all over the world, by millions of people every day. He will be rich." Luc paused and checked for his son's reaction to the news, broadcast before him for the first time. Richard was almost asleep against Cristina's side, his ears focussed only on listening for the trees in the wind, and we'll sleep safely here.

Gianluca unlocked his fingers and gulped at the burning joy of cognac. "I'm glad for Richard, of course, but why are you telling me this?"

"Because we want to share our good fortune with you. No, not good fortune, excuse me," Jean said, retracting, rephrasing. "We will be travelling for a long time and we wanted to come here first." He lifted the envelope close to his nose and stared at it. The words were not coming, not how they should. Gianluca's gaze was still aimed at him, waiting. "Your work, your creation, and Cristina's work since then," Jean urged, forcing his voice through the envelope.

Maman Sulpice died in the afternoon of a November morning, after Fabrice had left her to hurry home through a brief slowing of the storms which seemed to have captured Evian for the whole autumn.

"Tell me about the rain, Doudou," she had asked.

"What do you want to know?"

"Everything. I hear it, but I can't see it or smell it."

"I don't know what to say."

"What colour is it? Is it grey rain, the kind which falls off the hills and hangs over the water, or is it black like the clouds?"

Fabrice stood up from his usual chair in its usual place and walked to the window. The blind was up for the winter. He looked through the glass to the world beyond, saw the brick and concrete of the hospital walls, empty flower beds and the skeleton of an aspen, its yellow leaves littering the ground like footprints. The tree made him remember Manitoba, when he saw a thousand aspens spill their green or silver catkins as their heart leaves appeared.

"Well, Doudou, what do you see?"

The rain was not that of Canada. There the breeze would make the foliage spill rain in splashes, sudden pours even though the skies were clearing and the low sun was clawing through the lower branches to meet him. He stared sideways at the brickwork of the next wing. The rain shaped against the dull browns and reds, unremitting and characterless.

After three days in their company Jean-Luc and Cristina were ready to leave her parents, although Richard wanted to stay. He rejoiced in their attention, said "Italien" to everyone he met, although it sounded more like "Itahien".

"You'll come again," Sophia said, on the morning of their departure.

"Yes, of course," Richard replied, imagining from her enthusiastic, upward intonation that her words were a question.

They were in the kitchen, set in an extension at the back of the house like an afterthought. Each day breakfast had been an event, a meal which Sophia seemed to think passed judgements on her house. Jean was sipping patiently at his espresso, too shy and intimidated by the mood of the house to ask for hot water and a longer coffee. Cristina reached her hand to his arm and took hold of it gently.

"He wants to speak to you," she said, motioning towards her father's figure standing in the doorway. "It's about dinner on our first night. I can tell."

Sophia looked at both of them, her daughter and her son-in-law, saw the hidden communication and squatted down next to Richard to occupy him.

"Go with him, talk to him," Cristina said. She let go of Luc's arm and patted it twice in comfort. He stared for a moment at her eyes, dark and inviting, then turned his head to the frame in the doorway. Gianluca had gone. Jean supposed he should follow.

The house was longer than it looked from the front. Its high, narrow windows kept it dark and cool in the summer, at other times caught the heat and the life safely inside. As he walked through to the lounge he passed the ever-open door to Gianluca's studio, paused to glance briefly at the modern draughtsman's easel and the displays of pens and nibs, a space of straight lines and angles like the rest of the house. Light from the early sun was catching the shutters over the studio window and splitting into trapeziums on the floor. In front of the easel a backless office chair guarded two large pieces of paper, one of which was spread with various curls and loops of black ink segregated and sectioned on a lattice of pencil marks.

In the other corner of the room, still dark, was a desk bearing the prospects and results of his work. Two sets of trays held contracts and commissions, and in between them were a blotter pad and other small trays of envelopes and writing paper. A computer and printer filled the rest of the desk, trapped against a filing cabinet whose pale green metal was the only colour in the room.

Jean had worried for the three days and four nights since the restaurant, wondering how to atone for his apparent mistake. He could not find a way, or an opportunity. He was not even sure if he needed to. He asked Cristina to talk to her father for him, to explain, but she had only replied with her mother's name and silence. While they took trips together to relatives he had not heard of and whom Cristina did not seem to know Jean reflected constantly about Gianluca's image in the restaurant. He saw his arms around his glass, forceful and imposing. He heard the voices they used, 'Il Linguatore', a welcome, beckoning and deferential.

Yet you could also see that same effusive welcome as professional responsibility. Yes, there was surprise and delight at the family's presence, but a reservation must have been made. The manager knew his customer, his practised temperament. And Gianluca himself, he was a husband, father and grandfather. The intervening days had shown that with his care and caresses. In those paused seconds looking into the studio Jean felt calmer. The house was squares and corners, and the work was not. It made sense. He left the open door and went on towards the front of the house.

Gianluca was immersed in a vast, brown chair, preparing or pretending to read conclusions on the contents of a newspaper. Its contents were as fresh as night coffee in an airport café, the pastries given to Manes at the end of a day shift by the assistant manager of a sandwich bar who did not want to throw them away.

When Jean came into the lounge Gianluca stood up, smaller inside the house than out of it, older perhaps or less energised, a vague exhalation or groan emerging with his efforts. The smile which accompanied his movements removed any lingering obstacles to reparation.

"I'm not angry with you, even though you think I am. I will keep the money, but only for Richard." He smiled again, freely. "Look around you, Jean. What do we need? He will have it back when we die."

We. It was not his decision to make, of course. Just like it had not been his decision when Luca had taken the gravity of his father's name to his own apartment, frustrated by noise and its absence. Gianluca was the way he was and Sophia allowed him to be. Cristina understood the conversations which surely had taken place in the dark, the slow, suffused murmurs at night or while she and Jean-Luc had taken Richard out. But that is not to define Sophia as a monochrome matriarch, acquiescent and imposing, no. She is as much a creator of their forms of language as her husband. That is how their love declares itself in the white rooms and silent, shaded lines of their house. Not quite a balance, but an equilibrium, certainly. Cristina knows that. She sees their love, recognises it in the curls of her father's hand as he sits at his desk with his feet tucked under him, writing, imagining.

It is in her too, this space to sanction, to accept, to enjoy. She speaks to Richard with touches and strokes, sets her hand on his head as they wait for Astrid to serve them or for the school doors to open. Sometimes when she picks him up she carries him to the car for no other reason than she can. Yet at home, after sandwiches and a drink at his table, she lets him run to his bedroom to play and is left alone with his unfinished meal and the cavernous sound of his feet on the stairs. She doesn't need to speak to him to know he's there.

And later she can talk to Luc, after he has sluiced away the smells of violet ink in the shower. They sit at the larger of the two tables in the kitchen while she talks, or doesn't. For as long as she wants they rest there, her day and the latest school requests, complications, a fir cone for every child in the class, spare clothing, please, his name in clear letters, cooking ingredients, a permission form and strong, thick boots.

Or it is the trickery of the town, how long can it take for reams of her favourite cream printer paper to arrive, a trip to the bank but she forgot to take evidence of her identity and you know what they're like now even if they recognise you, can you give me your secret answer? A brand of coffee which was on offer but it's not the same, will have to be good enough for a few days while the cursor flashes inattentively on screen, at last a response from Cádiz but her Spanish is poor, barely more than a shared Latinate descent.

When the evenings come and the weekends she will only be quiet. She wants to speak to him but she doesn't know how. They go out together, shopping, playing, showing Richard the glides and turns of

58

contact on the shallowest slopes. They meet for long, social lunches in noisy cafés and restaurants with those same friends from the runs, communicate by peaceful sights and touches as other families and other children relate the vital information of the day. This is their declaration, Cristina with her skin resting on Richard, Jean-Luc watching eyes which could crush and gypsy hair, his reasoning, in the embracing company of themselves even while they pass those happy hours.

Do you see her then as Sophia, her parents' daughter, placing herself as the measure for Jean, countering him, balancing? Is this how they define their love, she in a soft, structured quiet and he claiming, stating, practicing? You do not see her as Jean sees her. Sometimes he will find himself at her feet, lodged in the corner of the sofa. Richard is asleep. Luc's hand falls on her, a sign, a tie, never by arrangement, and she will change into the shorts and vest she insists on wearing even in the coldest months. He gathers olive oil, waits for her half-turned on the sofa, cross-legged, the softest towel across his lap for protection and comfort. She will smile, adjust to his position as she half-lies, her bare heels raised to him and her arms across or behind her head.

The oil is warm, warmed. He tips the shallow bowl and pours some onto her feet, watches its heat spill first down them towards her ankles then be drawn up in his lissom fingers to her toes, runs small, gentle rivers on her toenails and pulls the joints below each one, stretching, adorning. Slowly he moves his hands to the rest of her feet, washing the language of her shoes away from her insteps with the points of his thumbs while he settles into the corner of the sofa, dark and as green as the mountains. She soothes to the sensation, a love, magnificent and inspired.

He shapes the scent of olives to her ankles, clasping it to the firmness of her bones, feels her tendons, their imagined power, holds her heels and the balls of her feet and to flex her ankles in large, freeing circles, concentrated and releasing. After long, sinuous minutes he glides to her calves, draws lines of oil down each shin and massages slowly outwards. Beside them the unnecessary heat of the fire reflects in glimmers on her skin. He holds her in both hands, slips each alternately in rhythmic grasps from the centre, round, in, tenderly clenches the thinness of her calf muscles and thinks of nothing but her and that moment, the measure of the lake. A reflection of a smile comes to him as he whirls his fingers in the concave space behind her bent knees and momentarily feels her tense.

This is their language. He pours more oil into the palms of his hands to warm it again and kneels to reach her thighs. Her eyes are closed, always. From the crowns of her knees he moves slowly upwards, pressing in instinctive, curling motions. He drags his fingers down the backs of her legs, carves soft, unbroken lines in her skin and fills them with the trailing movement of his hands. Her legs have imperfections, perfect illustrations. The flesh moves to his touch, squeezes of skin appearing and disappearing at the edges of her thighs. Jean does not see them, is focussing only on the slow flow of her. The free skin swells up under his push, slides back to comfort, oil and respite. He imagines the muscles extending and contracting, sees her walking on the road in front of him and watches the back of her legs as they near the woods, their woods, hears the time together and their passion like a steady sound from the fire. She is his love and his want, a declaration like the nobility of the lake and the water, like the distant calls of air waving in the trees or the mountains when they ski, a message predating and extending beyond Richard, climbing into sleep in his room above them.

He is at her hips, has reached the limit of her shorts and moulds his tiring fingers around the bones, stares without noticing at the shape of her thighs under his arms. As he massages the substance of her muscles her mouth moves, lips tightening. She is concentrating on relaxing, forcing herself not to react, a twitch, but she is becoming aware of the ceaseless stimulation of so many nerve endings. What begins as care, affection, changes to vulnerability. He will stop soon, she tells herself, summons silent urges to keep herself still and let him enjoy his actions, no outward sign of her tenderness. Yet the feel of the oil is warming, makes her rub her feet and toes together to relish the indulgence, and she loves him for it. She lays the back of her hand over her eyes to block out the light and disturbance and rests into herself, the quiet, his touch.

8
Geneva II

Manes waves to Lucy if they are both outside, drawing breaths of unpurified or cigarette air. By day the sounds of aircraft engines dominate the landscape, whether the sharp lightning cracks of take-off or the thunder of reverse thrust on landing. Manes knows them, could explain if you asked him the difference in tone between a 737 and an Airbus, even though he sees neither. The entrance to the airport, once past the tunnel, is the obligatory concrete. Lucy puts her cigarette out in the receptacle provided, none past this point. Manes hears the cars behind him and the city around. A parking bus arrives at the drop-off point, departures only. The engines of a CRJ short-haul to Brussels or Munich launch into final checks at the high end of the runway above.

In Darjeeling the morning mists sometimes last all day, when the spring sun never reaches the right angle to burn them away. The angled parking spaces beside him are full. Stands of signs say ten minutes maximum in three languages, none of which are his. For Manes does not have a language, not of his own. He was not born in Geneva yet considers himself somehow Swiss, but like the country itself he doesn't have a language. Nepali at home, English at school, later French at work, sometimes German or Italian, each of them badly. And it is not a call for sympathy or an excuse to categorise him, no. There is no reason to think of him as stateless or imagined. He is aware of his wants of language and is comforted by them, happy almost. Somehow it doesn't seem necessary to know how to converse, not at the airport. The bus passengers loiter by the entrance, waiting for directions or luggage. A steel and glass canopy protects them from the sky.

At the far end of the terminal, on the ground floor, Alain is waiting at the counter of the café. He watches the pale palms of the assistant blend with the black and stainless steel of the espresso machine, sees the young man's hands dart and flit in harmony with its function. The assistant works with his head down, focussing his attention, for he has seen Alain's eyes watching him, worries about their ferocity and their capacity for scrutiny. The company is always sending mystery guests, especially in the strange, distant hours. He concentrates harder than usual and makes mistakes. He has pressed the wrong button on the machine and poured too much water into the cup. There is not enough milk in the jug in his right hand, and it is spitting through the steam.

Minutes pass before Alain carries their drinks to the table, her coffee, his coffee. Lucie has turned over the first three pages of the newspaper and squeezed the muscles of her thighs together to watch her legs rise to the impact. She looks around to hear the silent wheels of a cleaning trolley or the cracking of bending joints, but there is none.

"Anything in it?" Alain asks, waving his disposable cup at the paper.

"Lots. What do you want? News? Death? Business? Sport?" She pulls the paper apart and hands him the bottom three sheets. "Here, take the adverts. You like those."

"I think your milk is burnt. He didn't seem to know what he was doing."

"Do you want the holidays as well?"

"Maybe."

Lucie lifts up what is left of the paper by one corner and flicks through the pages. She slides out a double page with large, colour photographs on it and glances briefly at it before turning it round for him. "West Africa, again."

Alain sighs. "They think that because they speak French there everybody wants to go."

The dark hugged them on the drive. As the car caressed the edge of the lake Alain had looked out over the water and up to the night, without seeing the moon. She likes it like that, as if the night is quieter without light, or if not quieter then more abandoned, its background noise more noticeable. She can hear the quiet longing to be seen, or could have done if Alain had not been with her.

In the café she will balance in the tea green depths and repeat sentences to herself, aligning phrases and adjectives in the persistent articles before her. She will make sure he does not see her, keep her mouth from forming the shapes of words. For an hour she will speak in the silence as he fails to understand that she learns her own responses, sees language come into her vision, fully formed and agile, like the way she finds her reasoning in the morning shape of his face. She has measured herself in the distance of his eyes. Love, she accepts, or at least his assertions. And if he would only stay still in the still of the night terminal she could recognise it more clearly, to her own view.

"How's yours?" Alain asks, swallowing away the bleak distaste of his too-weak coffee.

Lucie looks from the political reports to her paper cup and its plastic lid, heat-saving. She shrugs. He is uncomfortable there, she knows, but she smiles at his willingness to go with her, at the memory of his impatience by the front door of Jean-Luc and Cristina's house, waiting for her to put her boots back on.

Maman Sulpice was buried in her blue dress, the one with the delicate stitching at the hem and the broderie anglaise overlays around the neck. It had always been her favourite, and no one quite knew why. It was not expensive or especially elegant, and had been worn so many times that the striking cobalt had faded to a charade around the shoulders and under the arms. Yet still she wore it, every Thursday and sometimes days in between, carrying it like a history or a cache of reminiscences. Perhaps she had been wearing it when she first met her lover, used it to remind herself of the look he gave her in the rose garden at the water's edge in Geneva when he should have been looking after his sails. They met almost every week after that moment, he slipping away from the hotel where he worked to a tryst in one of the public parks or museums, never alone, never his apartment. Within two months their relationship was no longer news. Twenty-three years passed that way.

Or it could be that she had been repairing the hem line again when her husband had his second and final stroke. She still had the dress in her hand when she wandered into the garden an hour later and found him on the bench, a copy of Tender is the Night trapped between his left hand and leg as the pain reflex and muscle spasms caught. She finished sewing the hem on the bench, next to him.

Maybe the cobalt schemes themselves represented something precise, the colour of her mother's eyes or the complexion of her son for the minutes after his birth, until his airway was cleared. It might have been the broderie anglaise which caused the ritual, a recollection of lace and needlepoint, from the time in her early twenties when she would sit by the fire and create, waiting for no news from the front.

Whatever the reason for her attachment was, she kept it to herself. Yet surely it must have been some kind of emotional sensation rather than physical comfort to feel that familiar, worn fabric, to sense its acceptance around her curves and shapes so regularly. Imagine her sitting at her writing desk, carving and curling letters to her friends on cream paper, or listening alone and in a private release to Debussy or Ravel, the folds of consuming blue and the delicacy of the embroidery helping to soothe. You might even choose to believe that she wore the dress in Lyon when she first performed Chopin's

Nocturnes in public. But then she always loved Chopin, his beauty and his simple intricacies. You would know that if you had heard her quoting George Sand. "Don't walk in front of me, I may not follow. Don't walk behind me, I may not lead. There is only one happiness in life, to love and be loved. Remember that, Fabrice."

Each Thursday, when she was too weak to wear it, he took the dress from the wardrobe in her hospital room and gave it to her to hold. He walked alongside her to her grave, in the stale, concrete rain of November. He still did not know why the dress had meant so much to her but he was certain that he had been right to insist she was buried in it.

Alain walks through the terminal building in straight lines. He avoids the cleaners and their motorised floor-washers and polishers, takes aim from a distance away and chooses a route which will leave them undisturbed, uncrossed. The floor before him is the standard shade of beige-white. He has seen the same floor in offices and department stores. Lille airport has it. Brussels. Orly. When it is wet, when the mechanical cleaners leave weaves of slick, clean rinse, the floor at Geneva reminds him of the low slopes near the car park. It has the same used appearance, a soiled glow.

Lucie's skin has a sheen when they make love in the warm summer evenings, or at least Alain sees a sheen. He opens the doors to the balcony and goes to the bathroom, leaves her in the cotton safety. When he returns her eyes are closed. He sees warmth and accomplishment, their loving and his need for her, if not a completion then a continuance. She sees his nakedness, the combustion of his eyes, dark and severe, and closes her own for protection.

Fabrice took the job in the cinema to pay for his free time. He had the thoughts of his research, a sprawl of photographs on his laptop from the Riding Mountain National Park. He had his notebook, collections of drawings and annotations, the measure of lichens. Protections and customs had prevented him from bringing any samples back, and he understood and accepted, though he would have liked some small strips of infested bark. Since Maman Sulpice broke her thigh he has ignored the trees as well as he could. He left their messages unanswered in a stack of scribbled papers in his apartment. She needed his attention and his flowers, the walk past the old spa buildings by the lake and around and up to the hospital.

The terminal shops have metal shutters which slide down at night like evening descending. Through them Alain can see suitcases and electrical adaptors, beauty products, racks of books with which to occupy trips and journeys or time at the beach. When those shutters are down the concourse seems wider, more clearly deserted, and it is not the lack of people but the closed, colourless faces of the shops. He wonders if Lucie has finished her newspaper or her coffee, looks through the nearest cream perforations at the leaflets on display at the information desk.

Richard is asleep again. He has curled himself tightly into a single chair at Milan airport, where he is waiting impatiently for his flight to Morocco. From Cavaglià he took a train to Milan and his promised travels. The journey was quiet. Conversations were quickly completed each time he tried to talk to his father about Africa or Cavaglià, their car left behind, the smell of his grandparents' house, a new memory. He was bored. The train was noisy. Cristina smiled at him when he caught her eye, held his hand as he stood wobbling to look out of the window at nothing and everything.

As they waited on the platform for their connection Cristina wrapped her arms around Richard. He was standing in front of her, facing the track, and she trapped him against her legs. "You could have done it differently," she said to the space between her and Jean-Luc, standing beside her.

"How?"

"Somehow. You embarrassed him."

"I know. But it was your decision," Jean-Luc spoke carefully, a statement, a recollection of a conversation, chose his tone to discourage her from thinking he was accusing her.

"It should have been better."

Cristina is angry and doesn't know why. The days at her mother's house had been welcome, were even in retrospection the small, peaceful days she had hoped for to remind herself why she lived away. The broad walls and angled stripes of shadow were stultifying. She wishes she could have seen Luca in his apartment, inspected him like only a sister can. A train stopped at the platform behind them, the route back. She is still angry.

Why had Jean-Luc insisted they drive around the north side of the lake? What was wrong with French chocolates, or Italian even, that made him need to stop in Geneva? The journey was so much longer that way, and the autoroutes made her feel she was missing the tarmac beneath them and the villages they would have gone through.

"Swiss chocolate," he had said, as if that answered an unspoken question. "Your mother should have Swiss chocolate. I haven't seen her for so long. We should take her a present."

They parked by the water, picking a route between the coaches in the short-stay car park. And she had to wake up Richard, who had done the obvious, childish thing to alleviate a long car journey and fallen asleep. Jean led them to the thin lanes of the old town, where he found a chocolatier with the standard tourist fare of alp-ridden boxes.

"We could have got these in Evian."

"No, not those," Jean-Luc said, pushing her and her child-laden arms to look at the lower shelves of the display cabinet. She said nothing while he chose, nodded when required to comment on his selections. After it was filled the box was tied with a thin green ribbon.

She heard the station announcer announcing, heard and recognised her own accent without noticing it. On the train she heard a disembodied Roman voice tell her the list of stops, the next stop, change here for other destinations. The female voice's light, animated recording sounded foreign, as if it came from an Italy she didn't know. Jean-Luc was sitting across from her, facing her, and between them Richard was standing to peer at everything and nothing. She is angry and doesn't know why.

Her father irritates her. Her mother too. She wishes she had seen Luca. He had moved out, taken his noise and his eagerness to the blood smell of his new apartment above a butcher's shop. She was nineteen then and did not understand why her brother was leaving. She wishes she had gone to see him in the blood smell, the cut naked flesh seeping upwards like smoke from a noxious fire. He is older now, has settled into living within his price range of cars and women, a new model when the cracks begin to break through the paintwork or his low, mechanical whining drives them away. They email each other regularly, in Italian. Terrors have befallen him equally often. There was the incident with the brother of a friend of his from the garage where he worked, a misunderstanding, apparently, about a comment misheard in a Friday night bar. In another month of another year Luca had fallen in love with a married woman. A year later he was in love with an actress, had found her a place to live and a steady job. When she gave up acting she stopped dying her hair, he said. His next to last car had been stolen and crashed. The locks were broken and the doors didn't open. Cristina wishes she had seen him.

"What do you think of my mother?"

The train was accelerating again, leaving behind more straggled pedestrians making for the exits of another station. Richard clung to the bottom of the window, watching them fade. Luc's hands were on his waist, holding him steady.

"That's a strange question."

"No it's not."

"Yes it is."

"Why?"

Richard sat down on the floor, unable to maintain his posture.

Jean shrugged, an indifferent, ambiguous gesture. "I like her. She's your mother."

"That's not an answer," Cristina said. The boy near her feet fell onto her legs and took hold of their thinness. As he grew up her legs were becoming too thin for him. "Do you think she is too passive?"

"No," Jean laughed. "Your father," he began, then turned his gaze to the high hedge beyond the glass, deciding how to phrase a statement he wished he had not started. Had he been able to see clearly he would have seen that the hedge was starting to sprout new spring shoots. It would need to be cut back again. But the train had accelerated and he could not make out details of the view. "Is powerful."

Cristina laid a hand on Richard's head and stroked his hair. He looked up at her touch, moved his face so that her fingers reached to his nose and mouth, the comfort. "Yes, he is." She ran the ends of her fingers around Richard's mouth, turning them so that the tips of her nails would graze along his lips.

"Mama," he said, practising, would have said more, Itahien, Il Hinguatore, but the detached Roman accent warned them of possible changes and connections. The rumble of the wheels and the wind deadened his attempts. She smiled at him before turning her head to see the same hedge and its growth. There was no reason for her anger she could find other than the restaurant and the tragedy of their gift. She was grateful for the visit to Cavaglià, had seen what Luca must have known and never told her. She would ask him. Her father dominated them with his calm affection and his study. Was this his love, she wondered, the expressed definition of her family, her mother privately forgiving, presiding over him? Where was their invention, if not in their house or joint creations? The hedge ended as she dwelled on the white front and brown shutters. It fell away behind them to leave fields and industry, the impossible mix, and the awkward blend saddened her.

Lucy has replaced the newspaper in the rack, folded roughly so that its sections can be seen by those who may want the business or the sport. She throws away her paper cup and the last of her coffee, the cool remains of the night. Alain has not heard her whisperings, the declarations and permissions of her love. She slips from the café to find him in the terminal building.

9
Manitoba II

"You see, Hat, this is how it is," Max said. "Do you mind if I call you Hat?"

She shook her head. The last syllables of Hatsuke had always been difficult for foreigners, particularly those from the west. At school there had been children of diplomats and businessmen. She had grown used to being called Sukie, Sue or Sook.

"It's like this, as far as I can see. They get to you. Sometimes it takes a week, sometimes two, maybe even a month. A girl from Nevada, Vegas or Reno or someplace, they got to her in two days, the second evening she came up here. She was lying out there in the dark looking up at them. Said she was seeing how the sky changed in their moonlight, she did. But they get to you, these trees."

"Sure do," Diane added.

Hatsuke thought of the trees she had seen beyond the cabins, the balsam and aspen she could see from the window of her bedroom, swaying in the still breeze. She didn't understand what Max was saying but she smiled and nodded politely.

"It happens slowly, most times," he continued, feeling Diane interlocking her finger with his. "But it happens. We've seen it over and over again."

"Every year."

"Every year, like Diane says. It's one of the reasons we come back, to see people fall for the forest."

She's like a lover, thought Fabrice.

"She's like a lover," Diane said, taking over. She opened a can of Coke and took a long drink, slurping as the fresh bubbles hit her lips. "Everyone comes here to see them, to study them and learn about them, but the forest only tells you what it wants to. She gives you hints, suggestions, no more. All you can do is be near her, listening to her tell you what she decides."

"And then she's got you," Max said.

"Yes, she has. You fall in love with her, and then you're just waiting for her to notice you again." She finished her Coke in a second long gulp, turned the can upside down and shook it over the table, emphasising its emptiness. "And it's never enough."

"Never is. How long have we been coming here, hon?"

"I don't know, ten, twelve years?"

"Must be twelve. There's no secret to it, Hat."

"No magic," Diane added, in the space left for her.

"No mystery at all. You'll see, when you leave. You'll want to come straight back and fall in love again."

Fabrice watched Hatsuke's smiles hang on her wide face like limitless clouds, passive and conforming.

It was Wednesday. She had been at Riding Mountain for five days, including the Saturday of her arrival. For the first two of those days she had sat in her room, arranging the timetable of her research and documenting what she had already accomplished, notes on the setting, the accommodation, mostly on the people. The government body from Kyūshū paying for her visit was not interested in the growth rate of white spruce or the regeneration of the forest floor. Its desires rested instead on the links between forestry and tourism, on the returns to be made from constructing resorts in the high central mountains, all-year activities for those in need of mysterious, almost spiritual retreats. She was charged with examining the reactions and anticipations of the other visitors, people staying for supposedly emotive reasons, people like Max and Diane. They were the subjects selected for her.

On the third day she had wandered into the near trees and settled herself in sight of the others, seemingly absorbing the atmosphere and climate of the park. Kennet said hello to her as he passed back and forth with shoot samples to study that night. Fabrice smiled, tried to warn her about the changeable weather and advised her to make sure she kept everything under cover, but she smiled back at him, thanked him for his concern and carried on entering data in her laptop. He did not notice how she covered up the screen as he approached. He wished her a good day's work and walked on. His clearing was further away from the cabins. Emily was nearer. When he returned Hatsuke had retreated to her room. Everything was private in the public space of Manitoba.

Lucy walks back through Cristina's kitchen, past the small, used table and into the office. She has turned on the computer and whilst she was away it has automatically opened Cristina's mail program. A list of new messages is on the screen and from their subject lines she can see that they are almost all about Richard's font, requests or statements of use.

She closes the program. Brel is behind her, *Ces gens-là* circling outwards from the lounge and throughout the house.

"Where do all those people come from?" Alain had asked, as she drove away from the airport to drop him off at his apartment.

"Which people?"

"I don't know. Those people. The workers who are all still there, even at this time. It's nearly one."

"I must tell you, Sir, that those people there, they don't think, they pray," she sang. As soon as her notes faded she knew she had annoyed him. His silence told her that. And his eyes took on that callous, disparaging stare, straight ahead always, never diverting or aiming at the cause of his irritation. She recognised his gaze, focussed on the dark, dying tarmac. Yet she had sung, and the thought of that freedom made her turn her head to the window and smile through the glass at the verge across the road. A song, an unthinking rush of two lines in his company. Is this how I am, she wondered to the fleeing pavement? Am I now this person, here, in this car?

From the lounge she hears the repeated song. Before it ends she has checked the website of the Brel exhibition in Brussels to reread his daughter's words that true freedom is the right to be mistaken.

Lucy sees them again to remember, and to remember her smile. Brel will help, as Brel does. She disconnects.

Fabrice waited to hear Hatsuke's pleasant response, her thanks, and then went to the silence of his room. He had the day's observations to catalogue, the progression of insects when the sun was briefly at the right angle to warm the trunks, the growth rate of fungi, seed collection by birds and red squirrels, snowshoe hares eating the shoots. He had the shapes of light and shadow to remember, to try to frame as best he could before the next light and shadow. The room was dark. Even with the lamp aimed across the desk and onto his laptop the room was dark. He worked as he could but Emily was leaving his imagination and he missed her presence there in spite of the darkness. The hares and squirrels were active again. He could hear them trying to shuffle their way into the dustbins outside, securely fastened against them.

On three nights each week Lucy stays at Jean-Luc and Cristina's house. She does not plan which nights, takes her direction from the slide of her feet before the cinema or the sound of the mountains, unless she realises she has not been there for three or four days and the mixture of obligation and affection demands it. The house likes her, she feels. Its rooms welcome her. She doesn't light a fire but the heating vibrates warmth. Some rooms she visits all the time, the kitchen, the lounge, the bedroom given to her for her stays.

Sometimes she sits in their bedroom and enjoys its colours, the whites and creams of their world, envies the quiet they share. For those few sunken minutes she stares around the room, until the sense of invasion, hers and theirs, claims her back to the staircase.

She stayed alone, in spite of Cristina's clear invitation. When she was certain that Luc and Cristina had left, when their scents and skins had begun to dissipate at the far kitchen table, Alain came too. Lucie tried to cook for him but he had brought bread and tomatoes, olive oil infused with oregano and thyme. She wanted to make use of the equipment and the moment with lamb in red wine. They ate separate meals and he left, on her implicit request. They slept soundlessly.

Why should it be that Max and Diane would compel Emily to leave? As the lacerations of his studies healed in his notepad he wondered when the last time was when Max and Diane's proclamations were anything other than an affirming comfort ritual, self-perpetuating and elusive. Did they truly feel love? Almost out loud he lost Emily, nakedly mouthing her name at his reflection in the night window. The trees outside looked back at him. If Max and Diane's words were interchangeable, then were their sentiments also nothing more than formulae? How could Fabrice construct Emily, his Emily, against their deconstruction? It didn't matter then that she frightened him with her uncovered back and shoulders sloping up to the grace of her neck, hidden in the random shrug of her hair. She was like a lover, fragmented into leaves, branches and trunk, several trunks, a formation of ancient, ecological demands, and however hard he might try it would always be possible to dismiss her in a can of Coke or Hatsuke's bleak acceptance. He spoke to her as he closed the curtains. In a basement flat in Toronto Emily tried to reply. The trees did their best to block out the sound.

"Will you stay tonight?" Lucie asks. "I want you to stay."

"On the hill?" The phrase has become their shorthand for Jean-Luc's house, a code to signify their association.

"At the apartment."

Alain hesitates. Her apartment is hers. It is a possession and an identity. In Geneva the house he shared with Marie had first been his, had space and worlds which were his to roam. Since he had fled to Evian he had been trapped in the four rooms of his rented apartment at the far end of town, lost in its newness, low-maintenance, long-term leases with lifts and a low service charge. The hill house offers reminders of who and where he had once been, and although it is not his it is not Lucie's either. A neutral, informed location. "If you want me to."

"I do."

"Why?"

"What a strange thing to ask. Why do you think?" The perforated glass of the cinema ticket office is between them. It is Friday, the second showing of a romantic comedy he has seen before.

"I'm not sure. I've told you many times that I love you, but you've never said it to me. Sometimes I think it's just convenience."

She pushes three fingers out to him through the holes in the perspex. A glance at her eyes tells him to meet her touch with his own. "Alain, you're not a convenience," she says. "In fact, you're inconvenient. I wasn't looking for you. You came to find me, remember? Here, at the cinema."

"I remember."

"But that doesn't mean I don't love you. I wouldn't ask you to stay if I didn't."

"Then why do you never tell me, when I tell you?"

"It wouldn't be right," she says quietly, stroking the tips of his fingers. "If I say it in response then it would seem forced, unnatural even."

"Not to me."

"No?"

He shakes his head and smiles to encourage her to continue.

She raises a shoulder, almost in indifference or uncertainty. "We must see it differently, I suppose. I don't know."

Two young men come to the counter to buy tickets for the film, making Alain break the skin contact and step to one side.

"It's just about to start," Lucy says, looking quickly at the clock above her. "Hurry through, you should be in time. The beginning is important."

They take their slivers of paper and hurry away, a young laugh floating with them.

"I don't know quite how to explain it," Lucie continues when Alain reappears in front of her. The pause has given her the chance to arrange her words. They don't want to be voiced. "If I say 'I love you' because, or after, you've said it to me, then it's like I'm saying it out of duty or habit. It should be more spontaneous than that. It should demand that I say it, not be demanded of me. Do you understand?"

"Not really, but I'm trying to." He realises that he has been staring at her, at the looseness of her jumper at her shoulders, at her mouth

73

as it was moving, at her teeth and tongue. The awareness makes him blink, take his gaze from her eyes and move it to the wall behind her or the floor. His eyes are cruel, he knows. Their fierce almond glare distracts or threatens. He still thinks of Astrid at the café, the way her head tilted sharply away when she looked up at him, about L'Homme Rouille and the witnesses on the pavement when his inside wheel bounced on the kerb, their scolding, correcting expressions until he looked directly back at them. And Marie before them all. She taught him to look away.

"Fabrice will be here soon, won't he?" he asks. "I'll wait for you outside."

Fabrice left Manitoba with memories of the cabins and the trees. The sun had begun to break through to the lower branches, and on the day he stood waiting in the clearing to be collected a bright, verdant breeze was carrying light into him. He felt as though Evian was reaching out to him.

It wasn't that he was homesick, that there were noises in his head urging him to France or the Alps. It was more like a current of electricity, a charge repeating and reflecting home in the wind or the sunlight, scents of woodland, the sounds of a bursting spring echoing through the undergrowth. And yes, the trees, elm and black spruce reminding him of those forests still scattered on the lower hills, between houses, villages and towns.

The cars arrived at the terminus, delivering and collecting. He helped to unload them of the supplies they had brought for the cabins, as he had done every Saturday for the previous eight weeks. In the trampled clearing, still sodden from the winter's rain and snow, he knew that he was in the first departure lounge of the journey home.

The lake is cold, colder than Alain imagines. He stares down at the dark water with brutal eyes, seeing the threat it carries. Perhaps it is his city childhood in Lille, but he can't reconcile himself to the theory of water and pleasure. Even the years in Geneva with its delight at its geographical position have failed to make him connect the two abstracts. For him water means danger, the unknown, tides and currents to manoeuvre him from safety. Oceans, seas and rivers are merely things to be crossed in order to reach somewhere else, by whichever means possible. Lakes, of course, are pointless.

He can see their beauty. Not for himself, but what others perceive as their beauty, can recognise the slopes and shores around them and appreciate the cool contrast of their surfaces, but those are only distractions, symbols of their wastefulness. And there he is, standing at the edge of Lake Geneva, waiting for Lucie. Imagine his thoughts, if you can, staring at the night water, so calm and ineffective. Evian is not his home. It is a town which is not Geneva, an easy commute, a place which does not remember Marie but vaguely knows Lucy. How can he feel on that late evening while the film starts? When it comes to lakes he is illiterate. He has no language for his location, no method of communicating with it, and no way to tell Lucie how the bleary, flat shape overwhelms him. He remembers an argument with Marie, many years before. No, not an argument, that is too strong a word. A discussion, then. The sharing of opinions.

"You have no passion in you, Alain. Do you know that?"

It was one of those occasions when you make an effort, for no clear reason. They were at home. Dinner had been prepared carefully. A tablecloth had been found. Two pairs of wine glasses and two sets of cutlery had been laid out, one for each course.

No passion. If she had seen him facing the water just so that he would be standing next to Lucie while she smoked her usual cigarette. He loves Lucie. He has told her so, many times.

The steel frame of the cinema door bangs shut, like it always does. Lucy and Fabrice come round the corner, not quite apart. She nods at Fabrice, a gesture of connectivity and the compulsion to speak to Alain, and walks the few steps to the lake.

"You're always here," she says, sliding her lighter from the pocket of her jeans, "waiting by the water."

"You like to come here. I've seen you do it."

She lights a cigarette, a physical response. "It depends on the weather. If it's raining or windy, I'd rather stay under cover. If it's not, then it's something to look at. Have you decided about tonight? Are you coming back?" Her mouth curves to blow the fresh smoke away from him and out over the lake. He doesn't like the smell of cigarettes, she knows that. Marie smoked for a while, at the end. She doesn't know that.

"What you want, I want."

She arches her spine and leans across to kiss his cheek. "I'm glad."

Jean-Luc is still thinking about Cristina. She has not been the same since Cavaglià. Or before that, he wonders, possibly since he first suggested they spend some of Richard's impending money. They had chosen the destinations together, eventually settling on Francophone countries where they, or rather Richard, could understand other cultures. He was to practise speaking, to make himself heard by other tongues in his own language. Tunis led to Morocco and the forced seclusion of a hotel, their brief excursions to the markets carrying only disappointment. Nobody spoke to

Richard and he didn't speak back, preferred instead to hide as well as he could behind Cristina's ever-thinning legs while she was confronted by traders. He was invisible in his youth and silence, his lack of available wealth. For Luc the frustration of his family's sullen faces in the dry, hot air made him long for the comfort of water. The pool at the hotel tasted of chlorine and arrogance. They left early for Senegal and the wild sea.

Richard is asleep again. They bore him through the trauma of take-off and waited for him to relax into the window seat and the cabin wall, a blanket and a pillow replacing his mother's thighs. She too is asleep. Jean is stretched into the aisle seat, reflecting. Yellow ink smells of violets.

10
Evian III

She has not been the same since Cavaglià. Gianluca is commanding, Jean thinks, and hopes he will not be like that with Richard. He believes he won't. He remembers skiing before they left, Richard's growing independence, follows the thought down to the lake and the snow-taste of the water.

The cinema is finally empty. A young couple were the last to leave, hesitated in the foyer to put their coats on. Lucy has already changed into her boots for the walk home. In spite of only walking through the few streets to her apartment that evening it has become a habit to take them to work, a subconscious excuse to change her mind and go to Luc's house if the air sounds too cold or she needs the quiet. Manes has taken to wearing black trainers instead of his safety shoes. No one has noticed. They give him more grip on the damp floor.

Perhaps it was before that, Jean wonders, even before they had set off? Yes, he understands that the restaurant had not been good for her, that it had made her feel out of place with both of her families. But it was not enough to explain the shades of shadows in her eyes or the way she tied her hair back, surely?

She had enjoyed Italy, he is certain of that much at least. She fell into her language, the chance to speak Italian again, sounds of accentuated vowels coming from her like the humming of insect wings, persistent and heightening. As early as the second train he noticed their absence. He saw no echo in her of the other passengers' conversations or the station announcements. By the time of the flight to Tunisia she had regained her quiet, and though Richard was bounding with a consuming mixture of weariness and excitement Luc can still recall Cristina's quiet.

A steward comes to him and resets the 'call' button above his head. "Sir?"

Luc does not know he has pressed it. "Her silence is louder now," he says. The steward's composed expression shows no reaction to his unexpected words. "Can I have another pillow? My son has mine." He points towards Richard, snuggled into the window.

Cristina and Richard are quiet. Luc senses the air around the plane and the air within, the artificial pressure. It is tasteless, anodyne, has no effect on him. He misses the scents of ink and mountains.

Lucien sells books from a rented shop only two streets away from the lake. He keeps tourist copies of the latest fashions in three languages, sometimes four, depending on the season, yet most of his income comes from selling rare editions online. His father wanted him to continue the restaurant but he had no flair for cooking and no head for garlic. "You can go to college," his father had said. "Keep with the standard menu. It sells." Lucien took instead to a career, such as it is, selling the classics. Besides, the shop gives him the time and excuse to read. Once or twice each year he and Fabrice meet for dinner, struggling to continue a friendship which has not existed since they were fifteen.

Lucy is at the airport again, alone in the narrow columns of a newspaper. She is there earlier than usual, much earlier. Flights are still arriving although the last departure has issued its final call for boarding. She is trying not to watch the shops close or the airline staff seal their desks for the night. If you looked up past the edge of the entrance canopy you would be able to see the fuel trails of aircraft, vapour trails at their wingtips.

The green seats of the café give her enough protection. She does not feel the need to smoke. But she is earlier than usual and the halls are populated. You might look at her presence as a sign of a growing ease, a loosening. And that may be your only comment. The paper is creased where a previous reader has folded it to half complete the crossword.

She is reading the weather reports for France, Switzerland, Northern Italy and Africa. The lid is off her coffee, which probably means that she doesn't plan to stay there for long. Or it is too hot, or she wants to watch the steam rise and float away, and even if you knew her thoughts would they explain which? You cannot hear her, not with the noise of the terminal settling down into its soft, later glow. Tonight she will stay at Jean-Luc's house and she doesn't want to arrive too late. She should not have gone to the airport, not while it is taking in passengers. It's Alain's fault, of course, his and Brel singing *Le plat pays* and making her need to sense the mountains around her from a different location. Why else would she be there, you wonder, what does she gain from such a visit, when it is too early for her language to be there?

"It's exciting to see you again. How long has it been? Eight months? Nine?"

"Yes, probably. I was in Canada for seven months and I've been back for almost two now," Fabrice replies. They are at the deepest, furthest table, waiting for the start of the €19 menu.

78

"Two already, and I can't believe we haven't met till now."

"There's been a lot to sort out after such a long trip."

"Of course, I understand. I wasn't accusing you of avoiding me." Lucien smiles at his good humour.

"And my grandmother, I think she's worse now."

"I'm sorry," says Lucien. The strand of conversation appears finished. Their pâté de compagne arrives and Lucien picks up a knife to cut his onto the accompanying bread. "But it's so exciting. Canada, I mean. Tell me about it."

Fabrice crushes the edge of a fork through his pâté and delivers a chunk to his mouth. He chews slowly, allowing the simple complexities to activate his taste buds, then tears some bread to clean them for the next mouthful. "There were trees," he says finally, holding the piece of bread so near to his face that he could reach out and kiss it if he chose to. It is a fortification, a way to keep Toronto only for himself.

"There were trees," repeats Lucien. "Obviously there were trees, that's why you went. But what else? You can't have spent every minute with the trees. What other excitements did you find?" He scrapes his knife across the plate and removes the last of his pâté, eating as fast as he is talking. It has been months since he has seen Fabrice, and he is excited. "Come on, Fabrice, it's been months. I'm excited."

Naturally he's excited, Fabrice thinks. He finds everything exciting. It must come from a life in books. Without being seen Fabrice pushes his lips out slightly and rubs them against the sharp crust of his bread, savouring the sensation.

How can this man, this Lucien, be the image of the boy Fabrice fell in love with when he was eleven? His live, blonde hair has fallen to brown. His round eyes are lost behind rectangular glasses. Under the failed curves of his mouth and jaw there is the onset of a second chin. They are grown, of course, he and Lucien. He knows that he too is not as he was then, and is glad of it. Who would want to be as they were at eleven or twelve, left forever in that hinterland of post-child pre-adulthood?

And the love too, that had not been real, even then. Sometimes Fabrice remembers how he felt in the world they shared. He knows the sensations for what they were, simply that, sensations. The discovered ability to experience a transmission other than that of the boyish sharing of games. It didn't matter that the object of his discovery was a boy. He knew that his grand desire was Platonic, a kind of super-love, a supra-love. There was nothing physical in his love apart from the beauty of Lucien. But don't think that his love didn't exist, no. Just because Fabrice knows the reality or otherwise of his sentiments, their linguistic value, does not mean that you can believe him. You would understand if you had seen Lucien at eleven, those eyes and their passion. Look at him now, in front of Fabrice. In that older, indulged face are the same marks which once made him beautiful, yet you would only call him plain, as invisible as the words on a page of his favourite book.

"I was thinking about your grandmother last week, after I rang you. I had an 1867 edition of Les Maîtres sonneurs she might have liked."

"Sand? She's already got a copy, I'm sure."

"This one was beautiful, bound in red leather and with its gilt edging still intact. Very exciting."

"I think she's more interested in the writing, in the words themselves rather than the cover," Fabrice says. He reaches for a glass of water to rinse the bread taste and give him time to correct his insult. He has offended Lucien's passion, he knows, but cannot think how to refresh their moments. "Besides, her eyes aren't able to see the text clearly anymore," he says at last, replacing the glass.

"That's a shame."

Fabrice shrugs. "I tried to read to her but she says that it sounds wrong when I say it, that I don't understand the language properly."

"Perhaps her eyesight will get better when she gets home, to her own surroundings."

"I don't think she'll go home, not now. It looks like the operation she had has hurt her more than the accident." He pauses to allow the waitress to deliver their plates of cuisse de canard confite au cidre. She is young and certain, with a tiny piercing in her right nostril which makes her lighter shades of blonde hair shine in the bright wall-light at their table. She smiles, chants "Bon appétit," with the emphasis on the last syllable, rising, casually polite without being professional or bored. Fabrice sees her bare shoulders as she turns and leaves, thin black straps bisecting each to sustain her vest. He thinks instantly of Emily, her nakedness striding confidently away from him to the kitchen or bathroom, and shakes his head to clear her from his attention. Lucien, the meal and the subject of his grandmother reappear in his view.

"Perhaps I shouldn't have gone when I did."

"To Canada? Why not?"

Fabrice shrugs again, a gesture he has become more familiar with since the silence of the boreal forest and the noise of Max or Diane. "She was upset. She tried to tell me that I'd made my mother miserable, but it seems to me that she was the one who felt deserted."

"You had to go, surely? An opportunity as exciting as that has to be taken. Who knows when you'd have got another one?" Lucien asks, carving quickly into his duck.

A mouthful reaches his face before Fabrice can start to reply, but he hears the question as so inviting of a personal, private reply that he considers shrugging it away. Lucien chews and swallows. Fabrice changes his mind about the shrug and blinks instead.

A line of duck fat and cider edges along Lucien's knife, towards his once-beautiful fingers. "You still haven't told me much about it, this exciting trip of yours. There must have been more than trees. No secret assignations to reveal, no exciting nights out?"

Cristina is still angry. Luc tried to talk to her while they waited for their luggage. His phrases whirled around her like the empty baggage carousel.

Fabrice has his thoughts pulled back to Emily again, though he tells himself he doesn't want to think of her. Soon after he had begun work on his notes he considered writing to her. She was so involved in them, was present in the first twenty pages of observations as much as the spruce, lichen and wildlife. But there were so many things he didn't want to say to her and he didn't know how not to say them. As the weeks of writing and not writing passed the pages of his notebook grew quieter. He had visited Maman Sulpice and heard her call him Doudou. He had found the job at the cinema. Lucien's excited questions are becoming as easy to avoid as the waitress's shoulders or the widening spaces in the margins of his research.

By half past eleven Lucy was leaving Geneva, passing through the suburbs at the south side of the lake and hearing the low, metallic throb of the city's electricity fade to darkness. The lights away from the road became more infrequent. The houses were fewer, and those which persisted were gradually being fastened for the night. Bedroom lights were switched off as she passed. Dogs were silenced. In the small towns along the route the late-night takeaways and open air kiosks had closed. The bulbs at traffic lights and pedestrian crossings stayed green. By the time she slowed for the border back into France the one lone guardian of Swiss sovereignty was locking the cabin and heading for his car. He shone a torch at Lucy, saw the nationality of her number plate and waved her through.

81

Home, she thought, raking her teeth over the scar tissue on the left edge of her bottom lip, enjoying the sensation of no sensation. She didn't like Geneva, hadn't done so since an awkward incident with an over-zealous security guard on a school visit to the United Nations building. On such things decisions are made. And the drive back from the airport was always shaded by a unique sense of disappointment.

On the way there she felt something else. It's impossible to say exactly what she felt. If not buoyant then at least hopeful, optimistic perhaps. Certainly the deep tree seats in the café gave her a place to hide, a place to reveal herself. Those times have become ritualistic, almost a way of allowing herself slowly to evolve, to speak out loud in the repetition of news sentences.

But you may be making too bleak a picture of her, there or behind the velvet glass of the cinema ticket office. She was open. She smiled at those who smiled at her, repeated hello to strangers in shops. Like you she chooses what to say and when, how to say it, how not to say it. How to react and reply.

No, she is no different from you. But she uses the café for respite, and invariably the journey away from such recuperative moments makes her feel vaguely miserable or melancholic. And Alain was claiming her, somehow defining or limiting. His explanations of love brought borders of explanation with them, idioms and dialects which even if she wanted to she could not understand. They were not hers, not yours.

The night was irresistibly hot. A clear, burning mid-April day had given way to an overcast night, trapping the spring warmth in the air. Lucy turned the thermostat on her heater to cold and opened the vents, not wanting to open a window or turn on the air-conditioning. The road peeled further away from the shore, removing the chance of a low mountain breeze. 'Home', she thought again, 'almost', then 'Alain'. He would not be with her. She didn't like the way he altered his body shape when she was staying at Luc's house. It was her brother's house. It belonged to him and Cristina, was where Richard slept safely. On the late roads around Thonon, to the bottling plant existence of Amphion and on to the gentle hill in the high reach of Evian the car generated artificial wind for her fingers and face. She was still too warm, had grown hotter with thoughts of Alain's possession.

"I'll have to try to talk to him," she said to the front tyre, clicking the locks shut outside the house. Inside the rooms welcomed her, as they always did. Jean-Luc's house, his, Cristina's and Richard's. She turned lights on, took her shoes off and walked around, inspecting, checking, greeting. Something about the flow from kitchen to dining room to lounge warmed her in a way which the onrushing release of atmospheric pressure could not. At the bottom of the stairs she smelled it again, tasted the glow of her brother's family home, a building Cristina and he had helped to design. The trees beyond Richard's bedroom window were swishing in the wind. Lucy smiled at them, at the house's ambition and creation.

"Perhaps," she murmured, closing the curtains as the rain finally began to fall. She went back downstairs and made a cup of coffee to remove the residual bitterness of the airport taste, then settled on the earth-coloured sofa to watch television for a while and think more kindly of Alain. She had to turn the volume up twice as the rain flashed brightly across the windows.

Jean-Luc hands their passports over and waits for the usual inspection. The sombre eyes of the woman barring their way look down at them. Her hands flick through the pages to their inexpressive, unrealistic photographs.

"You are French," she says, in a light, amiable voice which seems to have no connection to her face.

"Itahien," Richard replies.

She crouches to make her eyes level with his. "Your passport says you are French. Your parents' passports say they are French."

Richard giggles. He is in front of Cristina, twisting from side to side with the found energy and confidence of an experienced traveller. "Itahien," he repeats, and lifts his arms above his head to search for his mother's arms.

"I don't believe you. I think you're French."

Richard giggles again, louder. Cristina sighs silently.

The customs officer straightens herself and hands the passports back to Luc. "Holiday?"

"Yes."

"That's fine, thank you." She steps to the side to let them pass, mouthing 'French' at Richard as he leads Cristina through.

"Itahien," he whispers back, hesitating.

Behind him Cristina is trying to pull a suitcase as well as control her child and frustration. "Move," she orders, then "Jean, wait."

She has been silent, frighteningly so. Luc does as he is asked without delay. He is sure she will talk now, beckons Richard to him and makes him sit on his suitcase against the wall. A cleaning trolley passes by, laden with sprays and mops and cloths. Yellow ink sounds come to Jean-Luc again with the squeal of its wheels, the yellow of violets and the magenta rattles, all peaches and nectarines. He fears a reaction from Cavaglià and hopes for it too, would welcome her restitution. The words he hears are not those he is expecting. They clash like the blades of a printing machine, trimming, arranging, organising.

"I want to go home, Jean." She pronounces the J of his name fiercely, like an Italian G.

"Home? To Evian?"

"Yes, where else?"

He takes her to the nearest table at an arrivals snack bar. Richard is placated and sedated with treats, a fizzy drink and sweet pastries filled with apricot and spice, diversions. Luc tries to find a code in which he and Cristina can talk safely.

"What's the matter?"

"Nothing." Moments pass, seconds of not quite quiet. She must confess, or release her anger. "I can't stay here. I want to go home."

"I don't understand. You wanted to take this year as much as I did."

"Of course you don't understand. You can't, because you can't hear me."

"I can hear you now."

"Can you?" She strokes Richard's hair, pulls him close to her to block the sounds and stretches of her words. "It's not just me. Don't you see? It's someone else."

11
Geneva III

The hotel is small, almost so small as to be unnecessary, yet it had looked good online and was only for one short night. Although the font money had begun to arrive there was no need to spend recklessly, Jean had thought, and certainly not on what was no more than a stop-off point, an intersection. Their room is adequate, functional, looks out over the end of Sandaga market. Scents of soap, wood smoke and rotting fish jostle with that of roasted peanuts to seep blindly into the air. Luc does not smell them. He is remembering violets, and her hair.

The two single beds have floral covers over cotton sheets. There are no blankets, not even on the clearest winter night. Richard is asleep on top of the bed nearest the door, away from the tragic angles of light permeating the closed shutters. He has worn himself out again with a child's vigour. That, and the time spent travelling, has forced him into a long low sleep.

It is late morning in Dakar. He is dream-filled, skis right into street markets and demands with perfect pronunciation the finest necklaces for his mother, a gold watch strap for his father, something amber and shiny for Lucy and perhaps a present for Alain too, reaching down to him and smiling with vivid green eyes like those he had seen in the gift sculpture of a cat standing on the floor next to a stall whose owner had pestered Cristina more than any other. The cat was as tall as him and had narrow, pointed ears. It looked like it had been drawn by a child. His grandfather could do better, but he only draws new letters, lines and curves on a page, and what use are they?

The ceiling fan whirls ineffectively against the late morning air, hanging in a stale stupor. Far away, in the corner by the shuttered glass, Jean-Luc stands listening to Cristina showering. He hears all her familiar sounds, the slap of rubbed bodywash, the rough scratches as she lathers shampoo through her hair, the swishes of rinsing, a regular line of light scrapes as she shaves her legs. The water angle and flow are different but her actions are the same. He knows the sequence, has heard it so many times at home that he could recite it to you now.

Perhaps it is the time of day or the location, but the language of her washing has changed. Why is she showering? For whom? It might only be that she wants to feel refreshed after the flight or clean the heat and grime from her skin. It could be the minutes of respite which lure her, some solitude and controlled quiet, an enactment of her own private volition. Yet the possibility lingers that she is trying to escape, to avoid the repercussions of her statement. She had agreed to go to the hotel, yes, but that was a practical decision. It gave a solution only to the immediate worries of flights and details, of Richard's care.

Luc waits in the corner, looking at his son's dream-flickering eyelids. When Cristina comes back into the room and sits on the empty bed he doesn't let her rest, wrapped in two towels. "Who is it? Why?"

"It's nobody."

"It must be someone. Who?"

"Why do you want to know? It doesn't matter, not now."

"Yes it does. It's important. It concerns Richard." Luc has had washing minutes in which to choose his sentences. His first choice was to use Richard's name and watch for her reaction.

There is none. "It's no one you know, and no one Richard knows. I told you, it doesn't matter. You're asking the wrong questions."

Lucy is swivelling in the old wicker chair. She has pulled it to the window of Jean's lounge and aimed her view at the rooftops and the lake. Beside her is a pot of coffee, a packet of biscuits and a pile of books. She has put a hairband on to keep her eyes clear while she looks down at whichever book she will put in her lap. Small threads of bed-worn hair slip past and onto her temples. The radio is on, the low resonance of a distant foreign language station. Its incomprehensible conversations will keep her company without disturbing her reading, a way of allowing her to keep enough awareness of the outside world to rejoin it when she wants to. The morning has come with sunshine and calm. She is happy, has connected herself to her thoughts.

"Then which questions should I ask? Please, tell me."

"Tell you?" Cristina replies, indignantly. Fast words run to her, phrases screeching and crunching through her mind, but she does not say any of them.

For a time they are motionless and wavering, like two trees whose branches sway in the breeze but never quite touch. The carpet between them is dust. Eventually Cristina remembers her shower and stands to finish drying herself. She unwraps the towels and rubs the sections of her arms and legs which were uncovered, her skin coated with a mixture of old water and new sweat. Her hair is tangled. Loops of black cleave to her neck. Moisture swathes her forehead, cheeks and jaw.

While she smoothes the drier towel across herself Luc remembers her body, sees as before the slender glides of her legs as she lifts first one foot and then the other onto the edge of the bed to dry her thighs, knees and calves. The sight of her feet makes him think of her lying on the sofa, her heels on him.

He sees the smooth ridges left on her belly from when she was pregnant. She dries them carefully. He sees her breasts and shoulders, her back when she turns to search for clean clothes in the unpacked suitcase resting on the only chair. Near the base of her spine is the mark left by the ski pole of a Dutch woman who had gone onto a red run by mistake and fallen across the slope. He knows Cristina's body.

It carries their history. She folds a towel over twirls of her hair and tries to rub it dry but it does not seem to make much difference. The room is getting hotter, she thinks, and I want to go home. She is angry with her parents for being who they are.

When Alain's car touched the kerb he felt the steering wheel jolt in his hands. The tyres slipped and gripped. Apples and lemons rolled in the dark charcoal carpet of the footwell and crashed back into the carrier bag. He remembered the sound they made, one in particular, deep red and angry, was able to describe it precisely to the police when they arrived. He repeated too with fierce, concentrating eyes how he had tried to correct the angle of the wheels and prevent the impact. The driver of the other car, a silver Citroën, had done nothing wrong, he insisted. He was determined to make that clear. It was his fault, a moment of carelessness or inattention.

L'Homme Rouille's papers were getting wet so it must have been raining. That would explain some of the motions, the gentle whines from the tyres where he would have expected an irritated cry. There were a few pedestrians. It was early evening.

He recalled the moments of impact, the way that his bumper had angled into the Citroën's low front light and the easy shattering of glass. He saw the driver's face, her image of uselessness. After that his attention was focussed on his stop and recoil. He knew nothing of the silver retreating under the pressure or its subsequent slither to the far side of the road. The apple bounced into the plastic bag and the lemons. Safe on the back seat were the two bottles of water he had remembered to buy for Marie, not knowing.

Cristina is angry with her brother for escaping.

Alain woke in the cold morning distance of his apartment, knowing that Lucie was not at hers. He thought about calling her, poured coffee into a bowl and dipped chunks of yesterday's bread into it, softening, soaking away. They had eaten together, quickly, before her early departure for the airport. In the shower the water washed the smell of smoke from his hair and into his face. He could still smell the stale, perfumed cigarette fumes, remembered Marie on his skin.

"No." He stopped washing, stood still in the hot pressured flow of the new building and let the water bounce a massage on his shoulders. And they were beautiful shoulders, demanding, carrying weight and power, comfort, the consequence of his build and the years passed in Lille with his arms dancing just above a draughtsman's table, muscles tensed and formed, a balance, an array. Sometimes he missed the days before Geneva, when his design of food packaging involved more than skipping a mouse across a mouse pad. If the office was quiet he sat at an easel again and let his arms and hands create once more, drafting, assessing, reworking. Marie adored his shoulders, told him many times how much she loved the curves of his elbows and upper arms, the shapes of his collar bones and his chest.

"No," he repeated, wondering if he should have left the door open to let some of the steam free. The smell of smoke washing away made him think of Lucie. He turned off the water, stepped onto the clean, brown tiles of the bathroom floor and lathered his face to shave. The mirror looked back at him like a night window. He remembered the storm, rain crashing towards him. At three o'clock he had peered through the curtains and seen rivers swelling in the streets, imagined the invisible lake to his side pulsing with anticipation and delight.

"No," a third time, "that's not the way it is." Water dripped from him onto the tiles and slipped away to the drain. In the clearing glass his eyes were dangerous, brutal, more so above the white of the shaving foam. He smiled to see if the expression would soothe their ferocity but his teeth glared in lipless wonder and made him recoil. The act of shaving was blind. He revealed his face slowly, concentrating his vision on the stretches of jaw or cheek appearing with each stroke. His shoulders and arms were beautiful, maintained their abilities in the mirror, their naked skin and shapes working in motion. Marie had loved his arms from the first moment she noticed their tenderness, sketching his concentration on a packet for rice.

It was soon after he had moved to Switzerland. He recognised her gazes, her suggestions, she recognised his returns. Their courtship was traditional and brief, unspectacular. Within months she had departed for his house in the north of the city, taken shelter under the Jura mountains and his sonorous, troubadour voice, his almond attentiveness. Was she mistaken in her reflections? Should she have waited, carefully avoiding his questions and kissing him to silence, or simply refused his idea altogether? She loved him, yes, the art of his pencil, his hands and hips, the broad pull of his shoulders, but was her love enough to act upon? Perhaps the act itself was its own justification.

And she was lured by his eyes, brutal and courageous. Yet his eyes are not brutal. They have no ferocity of their own, no clamour or cruelty, you know that already. In themselves they possess only that which you choose to give them. Marie gave them love. He had eyes of her love, as far as she could tell.

Lucy has had to move the wicker chair as the sun glares into Jean's lounge. She is looking down at the book in her lap, old fiction, pulling at strands of hair between her temple and her ear. Three times her hairband has fallen forwards. Each time made her jump.

She has turned the radio off. It demanded her attention even though she could not understand what was being said, as if the difference obliged her to listen more closely. She takes hold of a few strands and slides her finger and thumb along them, skin to tip, repeat. The manoeuvre helps her to read, each contact creating a slow purring sound to focus the text from her eyes to her brain. Her hand moves in rhythm with the lines before her. She takes her hand away from her head to turn the page and returns to the sound.

She wishes she had Cristina's hair. From her chair at one side of the window, away from the bright angles, she can see the road turning to disappear into the trees. She remembers snow banked up on both sides, slush-splattered, the base of each bank mud brown from the spray of cars driven too fast, even if they have their lights on. When she walks on that stretch she can hear the snow melting, complaining, ice drips cracking in the daylight. At night they will freeze again, compact into hard walls to line the road.

Cristina is angry with Luc for not letting her speak. She has beautiful hair, black, suspended curls around her neck. Lucy wishes she had Cristina's hair, stands in front of the mirror in Jean's hallway and pulls at the short strands of her own to try to see what the purring noise looks like.

And what of Marie, her sudden, invisible departure and her note? She is a name, a faceless history. There is only Alain's story, her effect. Her voice is gone, perhaps was never present. What happened in the years they spent together? She was happy, he says, held him and was held. Though neither spoke of marriage the subject was there, implicit in their embrace and conversation. As to the end of their love, there can only be speculation. One voice is not enough, can never be.

It might be that she became immune to him, that the language he used created distraction or even revulsion in her. Or the opposite may be true, that he changed into a distracted, revulsed version of himself, carrying bottles of water home with silent, sterile phrases. Whose creation can you believe? If she read brutality in his eyes, as she claims she did, then what or who caused that vision?

There is no certainty here, not in the failures of their love, the loves they declared. It could be that the failures began before those embedded declarations, in the moments of their primary arrangement into sentences, spoken gently and earnestly in the calm of his office. She was standing beside him when she first said it, he recalls, watching the fine pen in his fine hand jotting rough exercises for a new eco-friendly carrier bag, although he could be mistaken.

Maman Sulpice was buried in her cobalt blue dress. Fabrice waited to see if anyone at the service would read for her but no one did. By the grave he took her copy of Les Maîtres sonneurs from his pocket and opened it at random. He read to himself, silently, so as not to corrupt the words with his voice.

"You have no passion in you, Alain. Do you know that?" Since the understandings of his shower Alain has walked into town to buy bread and candles. He stood for a while at the lake's edge near the cinema, imagining Lucie. "She is real," he said loudly, his ballad voice carrying onto the surface. "More real than me."

An elderly couple in too-thick winter coats were throwing scraps for the fish. A stone at the bottom of the water changed into a crab and captured the larger, sinking flesh.

"More real than me," Alain repeated to them.

The couple turned their heads to him and recognised his expression. "Yes, I should think so," the woman said. Her smile was also real, as real as her arm linked through that of her husband's tan coat or the bacon in her fingers. "A girl?"

Alain nodded.

"A lover?"

Another nod and the shapes of an almond smile, natural and unforeseen.

"Have you told her?"

Cristina is angry. Richard is awake and worried. When Alain called Jean-Luc's house at the end of the long morning there was no reply. Lucy is at the airport again, early, earlier than usual, but she is outside the arrivals hall, lifting Cristina's suitcase into the boot of her car.

"What happened?"

"I can't tell you now," Cristina says. She watches Lucy pick Richard up to hug him, wishing that they could leave immediately, without the familial constructions. She is tired.

In the building behind her Jean-Luc is pulling his suitcase along another part of the dull, polished floor. He is looking forward to the train journey to Italy to collect the car. The quiet days will bring him room for sadness, and perhaps some reasoning.

12
Cavaglia III

In the coldest weeks of the year the snow is blue and silver. Not at the bottom, you understand, in the valley roads, and not in the ski towns racked like postcards halfway up the hills. But high, where the trees are unwilling to lodge in the thin soil and the mountains become truly themselves. Sometimes the peaks or angles seem so close that you could reach across from one to the next, if only someone would hold you as you leaned out. On other days they are more distant and more untouchable than the sun, especially when the clouds are low and have swallowed the brightness from the ground or the gloves in front of your face.

Yes, up high the snow is silver and blue, on the cold days when the runs are clear and dangerous, have ice-formed turns and skips, a sense of becoming or creating. Those are the mornings Cristina remembers most fondly. Richard is not yet imagined, or skirts on the shortest skis with Lucy near the bottom of the lift.

Jean-Luc is ahead of Cristina, always. She lets him go, watches his lines and his thighs tense and relax. She loves him. When he is almost out of sight she breathes deeply, preparing, and puts her hands over her eyes to readjust her goggles for the drop. The snow is blue and silver. The light when she moves towards him is crystalline, hovers above the surface like a welcome, and as she blends into the streams of the mountain she catches sight of him sweeping to a stop to look back.

His smile is what she remembers most, his excitement at her approach. They draft slowly to the lift in hot, sweated silence, talking only with blown breath and the occasional deliberate bump of elbows. Sometimes they hold hands as the slope eases to level.

Today is not one of those days. Slushed remnants of the winter litter the streets on the way back from Geneva, mud-brown and disappointed. Cristina is sitting in the back of the car with Richard, preferring his anxious sullenness to Lucy's inevitable questions.

"When will he be back?"

"Tomorrow, a few days," Cristina replies. "I don't know. He's tired."

Lucy shapes her mouth into words. A frown merges into her silence. She is still confused by the wave and eyes she saw at the airport. She realised instantly that she knew the man who had lifted his hand towards her, saw the cadence in his walk and his black trainers. After she had loaded Cristina's luggage she saw him walk back into the terminal and recognised him, but why had he waved to her? They had seen each other in cold air, at night. They had never spoken. Yet now he had chosen to communicate with her as she collected her sister-in-law and nephew. Speech is pointless, she thought.

Strangely, Manes feels the need to talk to her. Seeing her with others in the car park daylight makes him want to say something. He doesn't know what, or why. They haven't spoken before. Their relationship has been formal and unconnected, a recognition.

No, he considers, it is not a want to speak. Wanting denotes a conscious action, the measuring and balancing of alternatives to decide upon a preference. He has decided neither on a conversation nor their continued stillness. An urge then, an instantaneous, uncalculated feeling that he should talk to her. Perhaps he could have offered to help her lift the suitcase, or comment on the time of day and their usual meetings at night?

As he passes through the sliding doors and back into the unreality of the terminal building he sees Jean-Luc walking away. The wheels of Luc's suitcase rattle after him on the floor, silent in the massed noises of other cases and trolleys, the blur of voices, electrical and unsolvable. Jean had been watching from the other side of the shaded glass. He saw Richard caressed in Lucy's arms, saw Lucy packing the car. Cristina's form hung in the sunlight like a departing skier on hard snow. The station is a five-minute walk away. He walks slowly, not hearing the times of the trains.

During the busy day the busy concourse is cleared of its cleaning trolleys. Manes recaptures the two full bags of litter he had left inside the door and slips invisibly towards the next dustbin. "I have always been," he says, voicing the latest of his thoughts for no reason other than his own quiet. While Jean traipses with wonder to the station Manes is wondering, considering.

He knows that he acts, is prone to volition, yet he doesn't believe he is impulsive. After all, he didn't speak to Lucy, did he? And those previous actions, back as far as the choice of Geneva, the airport, before that even to his wedding. The speed of his activities might have categorised him as impulsive, a wild character who will find out later that he should have thought more carefully. His father thought so, and then his friends.

But they were the right decisions. Yes, decisions. Options and consequences had been considered and selected. He repeats that he has to believe his thoughts, accept them as his own. "I have always been," he says, removes the bag from the next dustbin and smells the sour spring aroma of a sandwich discarded hours before. A spooling line of yellow-brown mud-brown liquid is leaking onto the floor by his feet. There are no cleaning trolleys during the busy day and as he hurries through a door marked 'Private' the liquid trails along behind him like decisions. He will return soon to wash and dry the floor, but he didn't speak to Lucy.

When her husband had his second stroke Maman Sulpice might have been wearing her blue dress. It's possible also that instead she was sewing its hem, or sitting on the bench next to him to finish repairing the broderie anglaise. Or the dress might have had no connection to the moments whatsoever, been fixed in her affections for other reasons.

Fabrice did not know why the dress was important or what it signified. Yet he knew as soon as he heard of his grandfather's death that she would attach herself to it. He knew too that she would suffer without her husband. He had grown up in the air of their love, seen its consuming attention.

At home Cristina turns on the computer to check her emails and escape from Lucy. Words are coming to her. She is used to quiet. Lucy has taken Richard upstairs to play with his unforgotten toys, although as soon as he returns to his bedroom he closes his curtains against the daylight, just in case. He misses his father already, understanding that Luc will not be there to close the curtains for him.

"We left our car in Italy."

"Yes, that's right. Papa's gone to get it, hasn't he?"

"Yes." Richard kneels at his smaller toy box, pulling at the tail of a green dinosaur whose head is stuck under a helicopter. "Itahien," he says quietly, almost hiding the word in the sound of the helicopter landing on the floor.

"Here, you have this." He hands the freed dinosaur to Lucy, who stands it upright and makes roaring, growling noises and bounces the toy up and down in mock attack, the usual route to laughter. Richard ignores it and walks to the bookcase beside his bed.

"Will you read to me? I'm not very good at reading. Show me how to do it." In his mother's suitcase in the hall are the three books he chose to take on holiday. He stands still, looking over the titles left

94

behind, sees the colours and lettering on their spines. When he was very young there was a lamp on the bookcase. It is gone now.

Lucy looks at the dinosaur in her hand. Its head and front claws are a brighter green than the darker, tree-green shades on its body, the light browns on its thighs and back.

Four or five books lie on their sides across the top row. Richard picks them up, examines their known covers, and puts them back. He chooses instead a yellow spine from near the middle of the middle shelf, perhaps for safety or colour, sits on the floor with his back to his bed and looks at the cover as if for the first time.

"We've come home."

The story is about two lions, he thinks. There are pictures of two lions on the front, and one of the words above them might be 'Smudge'. Another could be 'Lost' or 'Last'. Lucy is beside him, still holding the dinosaur. She waves it towards him, brings its open, plastic mouth close to his nose and repeats her roaring and growling. The book is one of a series.

She remembers Jean-Luc having the full set when she was young. *Smudge and Tiny at Play. Smudge and Tiny go to School. A Lion called Tiny.* Luc wouldn't let her read them, said they were his and not hers. One Christmas she was given her own series of easy-readers, about a girl called Betty, and they were much more exciting.

"Read to me, Oose."

She snuggles closer to him and adjusts the book in his lap so that she can see it. "One day, Smudge and Tiny were playing in the jungle, away from the other lions." Her voice is light and free.

Cristina is reading, and typing replies. She is glad that she ignored Luc's suggestion to find someone else to answer the needy, pleading queries. It is her connection to the font. There are two more emails from the reserve in Namibia, one in English and one in awkward, broken French. She extends their permission in two languages. Most of all she is angry with herself for speaking at last. She searches for the address of the search engine to see the shapes of the letters on screen, hoping the sight will make her smile.

The terminal floor is clean and dry. Manes has returned to wipe the trails of his travels, takes a large, grey bag from the hoard looped around the loose elastic strip at the side of his luminous yellow jacket and heads for the next dustbin. From time to time his trainers squeak on the almost white floor, but no one hears. There are no spare tea green seats at the café. All the newspapers are silently being recited by other people, tired, strange faces he does not know. He exchanges a word with the woman pushing a wide, hinged broom in the opposite direction. One word only, not even a greeting, and each moves on through the day.

No, less than a word. It is a noise, a sound heard beyond the rattling commotion of the terminal like the shake of a snake, discernible only if you are listening for it or tuned to its infrequency. The woman raises her heavy eyebrows and slides one foot in front of the other. Manes does the same. It is enough to cross the differences between them, and the similarities. He reaches out to the dustbin ahead of him impulsively, counting its silence as another one of many, one more to tick off on his hidden list, his calculations.

Maman Sulpice and her blue dress, her love for her husband, his death. Jean-Luc falls into his seat and unfolds the freshness of a newspaper. His train leaves Geneva at precisely the right time.

13
Toronto II

Their tickets are along the left field line, halfway down from third base. The Blue Jays are having one of those years you dream of. Two of the outfielders are putting up good power numbers and with Dankworth in left you know that he's going to stretch anything to the gap in right field into a triple. First and third are hitting well for average and although Riverez at second is only running at .228 he's got a great glove. They're leading the Majors in double plays, he and Blake at short, and anytime you've got a shortstop on course for twenty homers you know you're onto something. Put that lineup with a right-left platoon at DH and three good starters and you've got a team. And that's the biggest surprise of all, the bullpen. Three right-handers and two lefties in middle relief, and the trade for Franklin just before the All-Star break. They had to give up a good Double-A prospect to get him, and sure, he's 37 and has had shoulder problems, but there's enough on his slider to save at least twenty games. You can't win anything without a decent closer.

Really, it makes you think of '92 and '93. You try not to, of course, but you can't help it. Nobody in Toronto will ever forget Joe Carter's walk-off against the Phillies. The days of Molitor, Borders and the like are still too recent, even though they are far away. What you wouldn't give now for Jimmy Key or David Cone at their best to shore up the rotation down the stretch. Still, the Jays are 2½ games up with just over three weeks to go. You've got to say it's theirs to lose. The Rogers Centre is a loud park these days.

Two foul balls have come near but not close enough. Emily loves the Skydome, and for her it will always be the Skydome, regardless of which corporate identity it assumes. She can't remember how many times she has been there, how many games she has seen with her father. Sometimes she wondered how much he regretted her being born a girl, for although they played catch and went to the batting cages together in the summer she felt she had disappointed him with her gender. He had been a good ball-player at High School but not quite good enough at College. Later she believed his passion was baseball, not parenthood. She was his excuse to go to ballgames, and when she accepted his reasoning and enthusiasm it became a passion they shared.

She is not with her father. He would not have bought tickets along the line, prefers instead the wider view from the bleachers in right centre, sometimes the expensive treat of the upper tiers behind home plate. Yet curiously, and in an unknown act of mirrors or synergy, the man she is with has brought his daughter. They have not met before, Emily and this daughter. She is seven years old, but so tall as to be considered at least eleven. The fact that she is overweight and sullen only adds to the impression of impending adolescence. Emily hopes that the foul balls will stay out of reach. She would hate to have to give such a precious treasure to the daughter out of politeness or equilibrium. Her glove is ready, nevertheless.

It's the home half of the sixth and the Jays are trailing the Mariners 5-3, one on, one out. Blake pops one up into shallow centre field. Dankworth gets an off-speed pitch on a 2-2 count and crashes it to right. Emily is screaming with anticipation, leans across Adam to follow the flight of the ball. She is still screaming when the Mariners' right fielder catches it on the warning track.

"You love your ball." Adam blinks twice, exaggerating the volume of her cries. He is thirty-four now, has given up his youthful obsession with sport and relaxed into being a part-time father. He and his ex-wife still talk to each other.

"Sorry."

"No, I like it." He takes off and then refits his Blue Jays cap. She has noticed how new it is, how unworn, but she hasn't said anything.

They have retaken their seats, wait in the quieter stadium for the Jays to take the field for the seventh inning. "What did Kathy say when you told her you wanted to take Jen to the Skydome?"

"Why?"

Emily glances past him to the tall girl. She is looking over her shoulder to the crowd behind, their murmuring nervousness. "I thought she might wonder. You haven't brought her here before, have you?"

"No. That's what Kathy said. 'Why now?' she said." He looks to his right, reaches an automatic hand to hold his turning child. "I just said that it's something fathers do. Besides, she's been here before. We all came together a few times when she was young."

The Blue Jays are tossing practice catches to each other, reloosening their arms. Emily stares out at the field, watching the third baseman and shortstop swap signs of encouragement, a hand gesture, a nod, the slamming of a free hand into a glove. The catcher is leading off for Seattle. He's dangerous, hits for average but has the threat of power. Emily should be wary of him, should be hoping he doesn't get the chance to extend through the plate, but she is drifting into thoughts of her father, a shared oversized coke in the bleachers.

98

"Are you all right?" Adam asks. "Did I upset you?"

She is glad now that she wasn't born a boy and would never have to learn how a father talks to his daughter. The crowd around her cheers for strike one on the outside corner. The big-screen replays show that it was a generous call.

"Keep the ball away, keep the ball away," Adam whispers to himself. "Come on."

"Did you tell her you were bringing me, too?"

"What?"

Ball one, high.

"Kathy. Did you tell her I was coming?"

He looks at her as he looks past her to the game. He can see in the depth of her hair and the stadium-lit gleam of her cheeks that he should answer, yet he doesn't want to. There is no appropriate answer, no response which will complete the weight of the question. Jen is next to him, sitting quietly. The Mariners' catcher hits a routine one-hopper to second. "We're good, you and me. I told her that. Adam and Emily. Emily and Adam. It works."

For weeks Emily remembered everything he said, every note of their conversation. She could tell you how his eyelashes moved and describe the touch of his fingers on top of her hand. She knew exactly how many slivers of onion fell from Jen's hotdog, could explain in close detail how the hairs at the edge of Adam's permanent seven-day beard wavered and wondered in the silence.

She knew too that the Jays had given up an easy run on a walk, single and sacrifice fly in the eight, and lost 6-3. Her throat was dry and the cycling air inside the stadium, roof-closed, was beginning to infiltrate her thoughts. When she walked alone into Liberté late that evening and met Fabrice for the first time she recalled the clarity of the air, in spite of the populace and their collected sounds and smells. She loved the Skydome and the Blue Jays. Yet she was always happy to leave the air behind by the end of a game, especially when they had lost.

It is a magnificent experience to take a train from Geneva, always. It doesn't matter if the journey is wanted or not, if you are obliged to leave on some affair of business or are heading somewhere you know will be miserable and unsatisfying, even if you have to part from that perfect lover, the one who knows your failures and misgivings and adores you for them, takes your memories and turns them to joy, challenges you, inspires you, delights you with the slow flickerings of their eyelids when they sleep, yes, even to leave such a person is forgivable if you can take a train from Geneva.

And it's not just the legendary punctuality or the cleanliness, although these things help, naturally. Nor is it the knowledge that whichever direction you take will carry you through wondrous landscapes, although if you are Alain and travelling east you would choose to sit on the far side of the carriage and avoid the views of the perilous lake. No, it is more than that. An amalgam, perhaps, of the efficiency and economical comfort, a grace, almost, usually reserved for travel in the past tense, a Grand Tour memory which has become everyday. Jean-Luc cannot resist snuggling into the luxury of it all. He too is tired. His thought processes have exhausted him.

She has not been the same since they left Cavaglià, perhaps even before then. The train swishes and gurgles along the north side of the water, through Lausanne and on towards Italy. If he had thought of looking he might have seen across to Evian, a swim away. He has planned to travel through, already arranged for Gianluca and Sophia to expect him with nothing more than his need to collect the car. If Cristina chose to talk to them, they would know. Yet the anticipation of the stilted angles of light makes him close his eyes, at least for the moment. His trip is undefined, left open to circumstance. He gets off the train at Domodossola and books into a hotel near the station, hoping the sounds of other trains and passengers will disturb him. He can wait for Cavaglià, and it will wait for him. Cristina is urgent and necessary.

Where has she been in the sparse, quilted hours while Richard was at school? Not at home, no. He can't believe that she would act out her dark charades in their house. He wonders if he should be angry. If not at home, then where? Somewhere else. It has to be left simply as somewhere else. Any further contemplations take him to other locations, other houses, other apartments, all as unimaginable as the one before. But he is caught up in images of her leaving the house and getting into her car, wearing those low black boots she likes to drive in, the pair with the wide soles for a better feel of the pedals and thick heels on which to pivot.

Over dinner, an everyday narrow, oval plate of spaghetti al forno, she comes to him in her second-best jeans, short shirt and blue jacket. It is warmer, late summer perhaps, no later than the middle of October. Is that how long this has been happening? Longer? This time she passes the car and walks out to the road. So it is nearby. Which way will she turn?

He sleeps badly, which reassures him. He doesn't have to worry about the confusion of deep, sustaining sleep, at least. Behind the

100

reception desk is a young girl with blonde hair and a tiny piercing in her right nostril. Were it not for the black sleeves of her uniform covering the skin of her shoulders you might picture her as a waitress in a hidden restaurant, serving pâté de compagne or cuisse de canard.

"Good morning, Sir."

"Can you tell me when there is a train to Milan?"

The girl looks down to her display screen and begins to slide and click her mouse with easy efficiency. Her hair falls forward like Cristina's does when she is concentrating.

"You are leaving today," she states, watching the screen in front of her change. "I always know when guests are leaving. It is in their faces."

"It is?"

"Their eyes and their foreheads, mostly. They have slept, and have woken. Restfulness and restlessness."

"You have a talent for words," Luc replies. His unused eyes focus on a stand of leaflets on the desk, see through the restaurants, resorts and attractions to the scents of their ink.

"11:07, 12:07 and 12:44. Those are the next three."

"Thank you." He lingers, absorbing the peppermint and trimethylbenzene, isopropanol, tangerine.

"Is there something else?"

Her black shirt reminds him of Cristina's boots as she leaves the house and walks past the car to the road. He thinks he recognises Richard's font on a leaflet for a trip to a glacier and cannot remember the request or permission. "Can I take one of these?"

"Of course, Sir. I hope you have a good trip."

Which way will she turn when she reaches the road? If she turns right she will be heading up, away from the town. Surely she is not going to the woods where they walk, break branches, take small steps? Amongst the beech and pine where he craved for her, wanted to pull her to the dead leaves and press her face and covered skin to him in that vital, frayed passion? No, that would be unforgivable.

11:07 is too early, he decides. It would get him to Cavaglià by mid-afternoon and give him time to dwell in Sophia's amiable, incorporating hospitality. The 12:07 train, or even the 12:44, will let him arrive in the early dark. A stop in Milan as well, because Milan is there and he is not, at least not yet. He leaves his suitcase and most of his possessions in the hotel room, check out by midday, and strays out into Domodossola for the morning. She is waiting for him.

On the pavements and at doorways he hears her language, her voice. Tones, tongues and vowels flicker across to him. Where is her form, the curled intonations of her eyebrows and the loose hair shaping at her neck? Unforgivable, he remembers. To the bitter shouts of a man to his dog and the slow burn of a train accelerating away behind him Jean listens to his words, because he has no other. If there are situations, he reasons, circumstances which could be defined as unforgivable, then the opposite must also be true.

Boxes of vegetables are piled up in front of a small supermarket, fruits from indoor farms or importers' warehouses. Stands of sunglasses are placed outside to shield the light, to tempt. He walks through to the wider streets of the town, to the tourist shops and restaurants, the bars and day-wasting cafés. Outside a shop selling mountain clothing there are scents of gardenias and peonies, or suggestions of them. If she is not heading for the woods, their woods, he will forgive her. Perhaps even if she is. She is wearing her second-best jeans and blue jacket, walks past the car and out to the road.

Emily was small. When she asked Fabrice in the naked cold of January what his first thoughts were that's what he said. Not short, but small. That, and the orange, yellow and red scarf she kept wound twice around her neck, just loose enough at the front to slip up over her mouth and nose while she was outside.

In return he asked her to describe Adam, unseen since they said a happy goodnight in the car park of the Skydome.

"His toenails were like flint." She was lying next to him, her head on her arm and her foot across his shins.

Fabrice waited. "And?"

"And what?"

"Is that all?"

"They were sharp. He had long toes with sharp toenails."

"You have no other memory of him, apart from his toenails?"

She wriggled swiftly onto her back and laughed. "Yes, and no. All you said is that I was small."

"You are."

"Precisely. But you must have other thoughts, things which you don't want to say?"

"Perhaps." He glanced at the portable television in the corner and the repeat of a twenty-year-old detective show, daytime nostalgia. "So he had sharp toenails?"

"Like flint."

"And the nails on his fingers, what were they like?"

She laughed again. "I can't remember."

He turned onto his side to stare at her, watched her shrug to confirm the truth of her statement. "Then tell me this," he said, leaning his face close to hers. "What was the score at the game, on the night you came into Liberté?"

"Six-three to Seattle. We couldn't get anything from their bullpen, even though Hatchem was gone by the fifth."

"Hatchem?"

"The Mariners' starter."

"So you can remember every detail about the baseball, but only one about Adam."

"I didn't say that." She raised her head just enough to kiss him and held it there, suspended, waiting.

"No, you didn't. I'm sorry." He kissed her again, lingering in their smooth warmth, not quite understanding what she wouldn't say.

She had told him about baseball straight away, given him the briefest of moments to take in the basic premise before insisting they settle on the edge of the bed and watch a game together. And besides, it was the middle of September and almost time for the play-offs.

He tried, for her, but after an hour and a half he was confused and faintly bored. It didn't help that the game broadcast that night was from the National League and he'd had to cope with the infield fly rule and a double switch in the sixth. In spite of the Padres' efforts the game was a blowout. Fabrice stood up and stretched, conveniently in the middle of the seventh inning, a signal that he was ready to leave. She yielded.

"They're not always like this," she said, putting on a jacket to protect herself from the cold as she opened the door for him.

He watched the padded cotton slide onto her shoulders and fall closed over her neck. Seconds before she had been wearing only a yellow vest above her jeans, and he had not noticed. "We'll watch another game. You can show me."

She hugged him and stretched her covered neck to kiss him. The solid crack of a deep fly ball came from the television, an automatic recognition. She put her hand on his chest and kissed him again, both movements combining to form a particular meaning.

"Tomorrow?" Fabrice asked. Her palm was against him, beckoning and separating.

"I hope so. Somewhere out, perhaps."

By the end of October they had passed their division. The Blue Jays had been swept in the ALCS, 'Another Year' the local headlines said. Fabrice learned to enjoy her passion and the World Series in her company. By game six he even began to understand what she had meant when she said that sometimes it was hard to love baseball and someone else.

What did she feel then, as she leaned against her kitchen counter trying to be relaxed, listening to him repack his rucksack on his way home from Manitoba? Had she accepted his leaving, as inevitable as spring training or new growth? That would have conditioned her love, if love it was. Emily and her scarf, her skin. Could you see her as that person, able to bracket her emotions, to add a sub-clause to something as infinite and borderless as love? The natural repercussion of such thoughts is to deny her love. She helped him to pack, told him where his clothes were. At the airport Fabrice dreamed of her reappearance like a lost language, and she did not come.

Yet she loved him. She loved him clearly and without sadness. He delighted her with the slow flickerings of his eyelids when he slept. Remember her, as you say goodbye at the doorway to her apartment with her hands clasped behind her back, not reaching out. She is the one Fabrice will want to speak of, will think of, in the low, tideless minutes of Lake Geneva and the glaze holding him to the trees and breaths of Riding Mountain. Her skin is pale. Adam's toenails were like flint.

14
Evian IV

When Maman Sulpice fell her thigh hit the ground first. Her right arm was holding a shopping bag, half-filled with luxuries which had become necessities in her widowhood. There were chocolates, of course, rich, dusted truffles which each took an hour to be eaten, every sensation dwelt on like the meandering of a stream. Less obvious was her desire for a particular brand of tissues, available only in selected haberdashers' shops, and the sweet, corrupted smell of unpasteurised goats' cheese.

The square, blue bag also held a book, for the journey, an umbrella and a hairbrush, enough weight to make her arm swing out as she twirled. Had the bag been in her other hand it's possible that her free right arm could have protected her, left her with a broken collar bone or wrist. But the bag was in her right hand, with its heavy, vital possessions. Her thigh hit the ground first.

She had visited a friend, not the imagined old lover from the sailing boat and the rose garden but another widow, a woman of similar age and position whom she had known since their husbands had obliged them to meet forty years earlier. To begin with her relationship with Madame Audran was polite and practical, a duty or an authority, yet their increasing encounters led them to build first a camaraderie and then a friendship. Pleasant afternoons were spent in each other's company, more frequent and more urgent at last, as husbands and acquaintances died.

On the day of her accident Maman Sulpice had comforted Madame Audran in the grand sitting room of her apartment on Rue du Colombier, posed amidst the burgundy cushions and straining elegance. It was her daughter that time, who never seemed to want to talk to her anymore.

"It's the way of children, Edith. They want to talk but they don't want to listen. We were the same with our own mothers, I'm sure."

"Perhaps. But she'll want to listen after I die. I remember my own mother, how much I missed her voice."

"Of course you did. It's only natural."

"I still do."

They sat and talked with afternoon coffee and the afternoon breeze from the lake, Madame Audran slowly easing into conciliation, sated by having been heard. Maman Sulpice left for her journey home in the light rain and circling twilight. She recalled nothing of the accident itself, only the walk along the pavement towards the bus stop, thinking about poor Madame Audran trapped in her apartment by the arthritis in her legs and the silence of her child. There was some contact, she believed, there must have been. The pavements were busy but she was familiar with the paces to the bus stop, had avoided the few obstacles many times before. Her bag had felt unusually heavy and she wondered if she had been more tired than usual. There must have been some kind of contact, surely. Her thigh bone broke just below her hip and again towards its centre.

Lucy has never seen a film at the cinema in Evian. Before she worked there she did not go, prefers to sit in the incomplete silence on her own instead of with others. And the films are rarely new, so if there is something of vague interest she rents it or waits for the television showings. Cinema can wait. It is no longer an urgent spectacle.

From time to time she slips through the exit door fifteen or twenty minutes after a film has started, when she and Fabrice have secured the takings and the ticket office. Even then she sits on the folding chair at the door, and her view is so acutely angled that the action appears slanted, as if refracted through a prism or water. She only watches adaptations or remakes, sees them in comparison.

Tonight she and Alain are seated at the end of a middle row, still close enough to the exit in case of emergency. At Alain's request Fabrice is guarding the foyer and the doors, and Lucy has only missed the first ten minutes.

"They've just met at the funeral. He's a politician, and the other one is a musician of some sort," Alain whispers. "He's trying to appear pleasant."

"I know."

The film is an adaptation of a novel by a famous British writer. Lucy has not read it. Alain leans across to whisper further details about what she has missed but she lifts her hand and smiles to stop him. "Enjoy the film. I know what happens."

Richard is downstairs even though it is late. He seems to go to bed at least half an hour later for each night that Jean-Luc is away. The wind is still and the trees are quiet, and we'll sleep safely here. Cristina lights the fire for company. She is angry for having spoken and sad that now she is silent. She does not know exactly when Richard falls asleep on the sofa, yet without looking down she can tell from his breathing on her lap that she cannot move.

It is raining. Easy, relentless lines of rain fall straight down, carrying the kind of sound and taste which tells you that it will be raining for many hours. Fabrice is under the canopy in front of the cinema. The doors behind him open and close, then open again as the audience leaves. He knows that Lucy will be in the auditorium, guiding out those who wait for the credits to finish and the lights to be turned on before they attempt to find their scarves, gloves, hats and coats. The worst are the ones who take off their shoes and then take minutes to fasten them again. The floors must be swept, the seats cleaned. Litter has to be collected and removed. Sometimes Philippe helps them after he has arranged and locked the projection room. He has the keys. It suits him to help.

She carries Richard upstairs, sits on the end of his bed with a mother's grace and watches him shift and settle. His breathing is sighs and murmurs. She would stay with him and listen but she needs to eat, to read, perhaps to float in the heat of a bath with some music to drown her. The main bathroom, she thinks, not the one attached to their bedroom. Jean-Luc has called from Cavaglià to say he will be back in two days. Richard will be happy when she tells him. He has turned onto his side, sleeps with his small hand under his chin, as always. Cristina can still see him and hear his quiet breaths. His favourite stuffed toy, a raccoon, fell onto the floor when he turned over.

What will Luc be doing for those two days? Where will he be? She picks up the raccoon and rests it on the bookcase, on top of one of Luc's old books. In the vague colours of light coming from the hall Cristina can see its yellow cover and the cartoon reflections of Tiny and Smudge. She does not want to guess what contemplations are squirming at the reaches of Jean's vision. They are yellow too, she thinks, as yellow as violets or urgent frustration.

She leaves the door open wider than usual. Richard is tired. He will not wake up in the night, no matter how much noise she might make.

"Here," Alain says. He has remembered to bring an umbrella, aware of the spring and Lucie's forgetfulness.

She takes hold of the handle to keep it over her. Their hands touch briefly, fingers overlapping. The rain doesn't bother her but he brought an umbrella. "Thanks."

"What did you think?"

"The film? I don't know."

"Did you feel strange watching it?"

"Not really. I've seen the end of so many there."

The rain bounds on the tight, dark skin of the umbrella like a rapid pulse, regular and ceaseless. He puts his arm around her and pulls her close to him, protecting, wraps the fingers of his other hand around hers on the handle. "The subtitles were confusing. They said so little of what the actors said. I know they have to be brief, in order to keep pace with the action, but it drains the colour from the dialogue."

"You can speak English?"

"I need it for work. Can't you?"

"A little, I suppose, from school."

"And you didn't notice?"

She shrugs her shoulders. He feels them move, one under his hand and the other tucked into his chest. They are walking in step, the way couples always do when sharing an umbrella, the only way to keep dry. The rain is vertical, at least, and in the narrower streets near Lucie's apartment it is easier to avoid than the wind.

"I'm not staying tonight," Alain says. Although he says it as a statement, an ending agreed earlier, Lucie hears the frame of a question. Perhaps it is the rain, dulling sound.

"No." She has a plan for the hour leading to night. Thomas Mann and soup, happy isolation, some bread.

They turn left at the top of the short slope, between the insurance office and the bakery, and walk along towards her building. Alleyways and service roads lead down to the back of the next street. As they pass them Lucie looks out to the hidden world beyond, sees the lake, the darkness of the other shore in the rain. The ferry is making its last crossing of the day, away from Evian. Its missing light has been replaced for the coming summer season. It has also been painted, but Lucie cannot see it gleam.

Lausanne holds its brightness even through the clouded black of the weather. Lucie stops at the next opening, between two grey apartment buildings as old as the spa. "It's beautiful," she says. When Alain stays quiet she continues, as if to emphasise the importance of her decision to stop walking. "Lausanne, and the boat."

He looks with her, for her. "Is it?" His arm is wet and water is creeping into his shoe through the lace holes.

"Would you swim across the lake for me?"

He does not answer. What could he say?

"If you had to," Lucy says through the drowsy noise of the rain, "or you wanted to get to me, would you swim to Lausanne?"

Alain looks again, more aware of his sight. In the distance he can almost identify where the town is, that strange border post marking the join of the flat lake and the rising land. But it is not a join, it is a division, the separation of reality and unreality, of time and blessings.

108

He cannot see the voluptuous water yet he knows it is there, hiding in the dark, rain-filled swathes of space. How can he answer her? He doesn't want to say no and deny her visions of romance.

"I'd drive to you. It would be quicker," he says.

Lucie twists her body around to look at him. Her shoulders fall from his touch. The umbrella moves in sympathy with her motion and large slopes of water drip into his ear.

"That's not the point. What about love or adventure? Passion?"

Passion. The wide, sparse rooms of his house in Geneva after Marie left. Her words to him before, her recognition, a judgement. He could tell Lucie about his feelings for water, of course, his spinning disquiet at its expanse, the inexplicable dread, but it would only sound like an excuse. All he can do is try to deflect her questions away. The moment will come to show himself and his passion, he is sure.

"What if I came to you on horseback, or walked thirty kilometres through the night just to wait by your door? Would that be adventurous enough?"

She looks at his almond eyes and beard-stained chin. A smile is there, waiting for her permission. "Horseback? That's a bit old-fashioned, isn't it? Surely that's a scene from a nineteenth century romantic novel?"

"And swimming across a lake just to get to the woman you love?" The smile breaks. Rain falls from the eight sides of the umbrella to the ground around them.

"I've never seen you swim. Don't you like it?"

The string of yellow lights on the ferry is becoming paler in the dark grey sky. Alain can smell coffee coming from somewhere, perhaps through the small opening left in the window of an apartment. All he can hear are the rattles of rain, surrounding, enveloping. In his right shoe he can feel the disheartening slither of his toes in a wet sock.

"Let me take you home. We're getting soaked here." He puts his arm back over her shoulders, touches the fresh rainfall on her jacket.

"Sometimes the water is cooling."

They walk again, the umbrella bouncing up and down with their steps. Her fingers under his are cold.

"Jean-Luc," she says blindly. Five paces, another five.

"Yes."

"Jean-Luc, my brother." Her fingers under his are becoming too warm.

Paces in step, the recovered shelter of the pavement and the sides of buildings.

She leads him into the entrance hall of her apartment building and pushes on the light. She knows they will take their places for the goodnight kiss, she on the first step of the staircase so that she can bend to hold him and be held herself.

Alain shakes the water from his ear. The hall is quiet, or seems so in comparison to the endless chatter of the rain. "You were going to tell me something, Oose. About your brother. It sounded important."

"It doesn't matter." She has taken off her jacket, holds it in front of her like a trophy or a carcass.

"Please, tell me. I like it when you talk to me."

Her hair is sticking up from where she has ruffled her fingers through it. "He swam across the lake." She stands on the bottom step and waits for him. He does not come until she beckons to him. "For Cristina." The light on the wall hums sympathy. "She wasn't there."

"Why not?"

"It was in the summer, and she had gone home to Cavaglià. I think he just started swimming, out of anguish or distraction, love perhaps, and then kept going. You could ask Fabrice. He saw it more clearly than I did." Her voice has recovered from the rain. It is soft and free, like a lover's, although Alain thinks he can hear something wistful and remote in it, especially when he steps closer to her and slips his arms around her waist.

She is waiting for him, for his contact. "Don't you think that's a wonderful thing to do, to have so much passion that you have to act in any way you can, even if it's aimless or inadequate?"

He kisses her to avoid her gaze and to stop her seeing him gazing at her. He has failed her, he knows. The wet collar of her jacket trapped between them presses against his neck, but he prolongs the kiss as a sign of passion or love.

"Goodnight, Lucie. Tomorrow?"

"Yes, but I don't know when. I'm having lunch with Cristina, and then taking Richard out. She needs to be on her own while she can, I think."

"Have you spoken to her yet?"

"A little. She doesn't like to talk, you know that."

Alain smiles up at her, a shared recall of their first meeting. He has weakened since then, become looser with his height and the song of his voice. Lucie kisses him once more, feels the familiar presence of stubble reaching out to her through his skin.

"How long has she got?" he asks, mourning in advance for his walk home. "When is Jean coming back?"

"A couple of days, I think. He needs to be alone as well."

"And then what, when he comes home?"

She drags her teeth across the scar below her bottom lip, a remembered lack of sensation. "He loves her, Alain. If she wants him to, he will hold her. What else is there?"

Maman Sulpice lay almost motionless in her hospital bed. For four days a temporary cast constricted the swelling, until more x-rays determined that the segments of bone were not going to move back into place on their own. She was readied for surgery, unwanted at her age and dangerous. It was doubtful that she would walk again. The judgment was pain, and the most efficient method to alleviate it.

When she awoke for the third time her mind began to feel hers again. She saw the clean cast stretching from her hip to her calf and was surprised by its smoothness. For some reason she had expected metallic rods to be protruding through it, a symptom she supposed of too much news coverage on the television, with all its explicit images.

"We've put in titanium pins," a doctor replied to her attempt at a casual enquiry. "Don't worry, they'll be fine. They're durable enough to outlast both of us." His thirty-eight year old face was soothing and believable. She relaxed a little. "There will be no need to operate again, I can assure you. For now, we just want to make you as comfortable as we can."

"What will happen to me?" Her throat was sore from the anaesthetic, making her sound feeble and in need. She wanted to go home. Not immediately, she realised that, but soon, away from the helpless invalids in the three other beds. Even in her pain and drowsiness she was trying to calculate how long it would be until she could next board a bus to Geneva, unpasteurised goats' cheese, Edith Audran and her daughter.

She was still in Geneva. The doctor smiled again, mishearing her thoughts. "We'll see how you are for the next couple of days and then arrange for you to be transferred to Evian. If the pain is bad, press this button," he said, positioning the morphine line on her stomach. "I'll come and see you later. The nurses will help with everything else."

With everything else. If the pain is bad. "What day is it?"

"Sunday."

She had missed her day to wear her dress. More than anything else, even more than her husband or an unbroken leg, she wanted to feel the cobalt blue against her arms, sense the broderie anglaise around her neck.

Lucy rests her jacket on the back of a chair to dry. A packet of broccoli and cauliflower soup is simmering on the stove. Steam swirls up, like light. She is reclaiming silence, thinking about Alain and Jean-Luc and Cristina as she chops ham to add to the soup. He doesn't hear me, she thinks, doesn't have the will sometimes to try to listen more closely. She cuts thick bread into thin slices to make complicated flavours, each one subtle and unique, adds salt and pepper, white not black, basil and chives, fetches her book from the clamour of the bedroom and clears space on the table. A welcome tiredness is in the smells from the stove and the firm, soft centres of the bread, arranged in a row on a plate.

She pours her soup into a bowl and wonders whether Alain wants to recognise her cries and whispers for what they are when she reveals them. The thought irritates her so much that she opens the curtains and her book as distractions. She eats slowly, savouring the words. The rain is persistent enough to be unheard.

15
Amsterdam

Cristina is asleep on the wrong side of the bed. The rain falls like lights or echoes. In the morning she will wonder if she dreamt at all, will make breakfast for Richard then wait for him to come home again at lunchtime. She was surprised at how eager and conciliatory the school had seemed, happy to accept him back, almost apologetic for his leaving. "Schooh," he says, and "Itahien." She will wait at home for him. Evian is too busy, too filled with potential. The tourists are returning, with strange, tourist voices.

She is on top of the covers in her bathrobe. The sheets have lost the smell of her husband. Two towels are making the carpet damp. Bulbs are still on in the bathroom and on the landing, shining a slither into Richard's quiet room. A lamp on her bedside table illuminates the fragments of water still in her hair. On her left ankle there is a small strand of dried blood and the skin on her thighs is waiting for moisturiser. Somewhere in her sleep is the memory of tears.

Even though she is tired Lucy is aware of Alain, feels the difference, cannot sleep. Perhaps she is too tired, or only physically tired. She lies in the pallid darkness of her bed and turns the radio on, but the liquid chatter and aimless music soon merge into the silence of the room. Although she had said nothing, to protect him and their evening, she hadn't liked the film. It had been too morose for her, too predictable, too full of human frailty. And behind her reasons, sustaining them, was the knowledge that she hadn't enjoyed the experience of watching a film at the cinema. There was a stain of infidelity about it, the constant thought that she should be counting cents in the ticket office or outside with Fabrice, letting the singles and couples inside care for their own desires.

She thinks about turning the light on and going to wash her face. Perhaps cool water will subdue her. She had eaten her soup and read her book, pausing occasionally with the spoon halfway to her mouth to look out at the falling lines of rain. There was comfort in that, at least, the warming silence and hot food. Alain had tried to please her, she knew, and it wasn't his fault. She dismissed their conversation on the way home as a symptom, nothing more. He could not be more than himself.

The day had begun with disconnection and it had led her through. In the bathroom the light is bright and the water flowing from the taps is loud. She sees herself in the mirror, the loose-cut brown bed-ridden hair, her eyebrows in need of work as always, her small, symmetrical nose. She likes her mouth, wide and curving upwards like her father's. It is almost a mouth to be proud of. But whose mouth does Alain have? Where does his skin come from?

Around the corners of her eyes are intimations of age. She rubs in some night cream, remembering the dirt of Geneva, the lifeless air, their attempts to speak that morning. She had woken up in a lost, reflective mood, and over breakfast she had the feeling that she should be somewhere, talking to someone, but she didn't know where or who. The apartment was too small and too big. There were clothes on the bedroom floor, half-worn jeans and jumpers, socks, two vests and her fawn shirt. The clock on the stove flashed zeros at her from another interruption in the electricity supply. She had run out of good coffee and couldn't gather the energy to go out and get some more.

She was contained by the main room, stared at the corner sofa opposite the corner kitchen, not wanting to sit down. It was too cold to stand on the balcony. The street below had to wait for the sun to rise higher over the mountains to get a more useful view. Evian was always cold in the mornings, even in summer, but when at last the glare was directed it was quick and hot. The tables outside the cafés would be filled with tourists while the residents stayed in shaded interiors. Shops would close their blinds for lunch and not reopen them for afternoon trade.

Heat came quickly, from the water and the sheer, unpolluted sky. Summer was too constrained, Lucy thought, compared to the urge to action of spring and autumn. She opened the balcony doors to her disquiet and let the flow of the morning overwhelm her. By eleven o'clock the restrictions of her apartment had made her restless and frustrated. She wished it was late enough for her to drive to the tea green seats of the airport and a used newspaper, release herself in other people's words already read by other people. She called Alain at work and pleaded with him to let her meet him for lunch. Geneva was at least different. He was not the airport or silence, yet he was not her managed, comfortable rooms with their order and limitation. She could take her stupor there and be herself, however that was, and no one would notice.

"What's wrong? You sounded upset when you called, almost desperate, as if you had banged your foot against the leg of a chair and were trying not to let the pain get to your brain."

"That's the strangest thing I've ever heard you say." Lucie remembered the words she had used but not the intonation. She might have sounded awkward, she realised, clumsy and dishevelled.

He only had an hour for lunch, and with the walking that had shrunk to forty minutes. He queued for them both at the counter of a snack bar while she struggled for a table. When she claimed one it was still littered with the debris of another rushed lunch. She pushed the three plates to one corner of the plastic practicality and wiped a serviette over the space. Crumbs and liquid gathered at the table's silver lip.

Alain put his sandwich down and sat opposite her. Usually he didn't eat lunch but she had asked to meet him. "I got you a coffee," he said, pushing a large, yellow cup towards her.

"Thanks." The dark surface was already staining the rim, at a height where a thin white stripe ran around the outside.

"Are you going to tell me why you came, what this is all about? We never have lunch during the week."

"I don't know."

"You don't know why you came or you don't know if you're going to tell me?"

"Yes. No. Yes and no. Both. Stop confusing me, Alain."

"I was only trying to cheer you up. You look concerned."

"I wanted to see you," she said, looking at the yellow handle of the cup, seeing only the white inside.

"And you have, and now you're upset."

"I said I wanted to see you, not talk to you."

"Then let's not talk, if that's what you want."

She watched his intricate fingers curl and grasp as he picked up the sandwich. They were as amber as his face, showed signs of cruelty amidst the delicacy and touch, a show perhaps of the capability for destruction. She liked his hands, or rather she liked being held by them. Who would not want to be held, securely and tenderly? Yet his hands softly holding the sandwich as he chewed then bringing it up to his face to tear another mouthful of tomatoes and two cheeses, those lithe, draughtsman's wrists and solid forearms, they all seemed to be part of someone else, another Alain. It was her mood, she thought, that same impatience which had led her to him.

Her gaze fell back to the yellow cup before her, its skin like the stale spring sun. "I'm sorry, Alain." She scratched the top of her head roughly, her palm pressed against her forehead. "Talk to me, please."

He lowered the strains of Savoie cheese, the skin of tomatoes. "I'd like to. I don't know what to say."

"Say anything. I want to hear your voice."

"How do I know I won't upset you again?" he asked, lowering his tone to that soft balladeer's voice, a moveable echo. When she didn't reply immediately he stayed silent, noticing the temperature.

She sipped at her coffee. It was already too cold. "I don't want Jean-Luc to be away. I want him to be at home," she said, and immediately regretted it. Her disquiet was open and free, spoken, voiced. The words were new. She didn't know they were hers.

Manes has looked for Lucy every day since they almost met. He slows his trolley to a rumble and searches the shapes in the café when he walks past. In the shelter of the glass and steel canopy he wanders in the dark, clear air, hoping to find her there. He doesn't know if he will speak to her, has decided not to but realises he is impetuous, or could be seen as so. A nod, certainly, a vague inclination of his head or eyes, the recognition of recognition.

What would he say if he spoke to her? He has returned to the slow comfort of nights. The terminal lights gleam more brightly at him, almost mocking. Their reflections bound from the windows and the floor like echoes. Without the threads of travellers filling the concourse with their queues and time-consuming ambles the airport is fierce and brutal, yet Manes prefers the overnight shifts. He has time to think about the day almost completed and the one to come, wages earned and spent or allotted.

Manjusha wakes him at lunchtime. She brings him tea and breakfast and tells him about her morning, the routine of getting his daughters to school and the places she has taken two year old Akash to amuse him. She is always out in the morning. Sometimes she goes shopping or visits one of the two other Indian families they know in Geneva, anything to make sure that Manes can sleep through the beckoning daylight. She is tall, not quite too tall. Her body has learnt how to carry children, both before and after birth. It swims and sways with them, the palms of her hands and her hips attuned to them. Her eyes miss the tea steppes of Darjeeling. They will go back one day, she knows, and see the mist like a breath or a caution. Her skin will welcome its warm, wet embrace.

After breakfast Manes concentrates on his carving for at least an hour every afternoon. The action makes him prepare for the rest of the day. He only has a few basic tools but can create delicate patterns in teak, mahogany or rosewood. They talk to him, these cheaper off-cuts. They tell him ancient stories like those his mother once told, histories of gods and battles. Other tales too, ones he has learned for himself from the books and televisions of Switzerland and France.

You could see Hannibal on a square of mahogany, if he would show it to you, or flick through images of Lakshmi and Ganesh to look at Alexander burning Persepolis. He has carved the Parthenon into rosewood, chipped slivers of pale, faulted teak away to leave a picture of the Matterhorn rising at the sky like a broken claw, but he will not let you see it. The practice is for him only, and for Manjusha. She comforts him when they don't look how he wants them to, tells him that his father would be proud if he knew that he was still using his abilities.

The action prepares him. It relaxes his muscles and eyes to their memorised attention. When the girls are home he plays with his children and eats, another night of floors, walls, toilets and dustbins, one more closer to an ending. He doesn't know what he will say to Lucy if he speaks to her. He thinks that he won't but Manjusha knows he is impetuous. The words cannot be decided upon in advance.

"You're worried about your brother."

"Of course I am. And Cristina and Richard." Lucy wished her coffee was hot. It would have been something to hide behind.

Alain bit a response, chewed slowly. The woman in front of him was not Marie, but she would have understood. Not then, but later, afterwards. "Yes," he said. He could think of nothing else. "Is that why you wanted to meet me? To stop thinking for a while?"

"I don't know, maybe. I wanted to talk to somebody, someone I know. Not about Luc and Cristina."

He put down the last third of his sandwich and licked the fingers of his right hand as he leaned towards her. They tasted bitter and sweet. "I had a car crash once, when I still lived here. It wasn't serious, just a slide on a wet road, but when I got home there was no one to talk to. All day at the office we talk to each other, meaningless noise to help us concentrate. It means nothing."

"We are a million laughing at the million facing us, but two million laughs don't prevent us finding ourselves alone again in the mirror."

"I'm not sure I agree."

"No?"

"Sometimes, not always. But that's pretty. Baudelaire? Rilke?"

"Brel."

He sat up again, grasped the last crushed remains of his lunch and looked at his watch. He only had fifteen minutes to get back to work. "It's still pretty. But I'm sure it sounds better when you say it than when he sings it."

She heard that his voice had gone. The low, somnolent caresses had been replaced with indifference, and it annoyed her.

Maman Sulpice was buried in her blue dress, at Fabrice's insistence. He has been thinking about her, or more specifically, about death. Not in a morbid, preoccupied contemplation of mortality but rather about endings, the silence which has rushed to him as secretly and completely as early light. Since meeting Lucien for dinner his image of himself has changed, shrunken into a solitary figure at a keyboard, investigating, recalling, reciting. The notes and observations of Manitoba live through him. White spruce and aspen, balsam fir, the lifecycles of lichen and peculiar fungi, their need for regeneration and regrowth.

He has decided to visit her, although he has to be at work early as he has promised Alain that he and Lucy can watch the film together. Maman Sulpice's headstone looks too new. Its white granite sheen is out of place amongst the greying neighbours. He has almost finished the final draft of his research. It is cold and impassive, sentences and diagrams which seem to have no connection to his personal experiences. The thought of finishing carries its own lethargy. He doesn't want to be consumed by his work, led into the secluded glades of similar and obvious projects. The passion, if that is what it was, has left him. Or he left it, he thinks. He has arrived at an ending.

"Doudou," he hears her say, "you've come to visit me. I wish I could see you clearly. Tell me, what do you look like?"

It is the opening day of the baseball season. He had promised to remember the date, rubs his hand along the curved top of the headstone as he keeps the promise. He will look to see the result of the Blue Jays' first game, and no more. 'Amantine Aurore Lucile Sulpice', and underneath 'Loving Wife'. That was all she had wanted. But she is beside her husband and in her cobalt blue dress.

Opening Day. A great event. He remembers Max and Diane chanting their devotion to the Milwaukee Brewers. "It's like a lover," Max said over the standard breakfast of granola, eggs, bacon and toast. "You can't get away, even if you want to. The team gets to you, with all its disappointment and hope."

"And you'll be with them through thick and thin," Diane added. "Wherever you go in the world they'll be with you. Look at us all the way up here, and we still can't get those damn Brewers out of our thinking."

"No way."

"No way. I can't wait for Opening Day, to fall for them all over again."

118

Fabrice said nothing. He cleared away his plate and washed up his cup, smiling at them to show he understood. It was the quickest way to leave them, he had learned. Hatsuke had showed him that.

In his small clearing between three trees he unpacked his camera and notebook and wondered if they knew that they were wrong about him, that the forest had not got to him. Did they care? He was there to gather research. Love, or more appropriately for Max and Diane a passionate enchantment, was not going to delay him while he worked. Rain begins to fall. The gravel paths are changing colour. He didn't mention the Toronto Blue Jays, either at Riding Mountain or in Evian. Maman Sulpice would recognise his privacy. She would not ask why.

"Stop being cruel, Alain, just because you can."

Cruel. He blinked and looked away, deliberately softening. "I have to get back to the office. Will you walk with me?"

On the street they walked at her pace even though it would make him late. He had earned that right, he thought, once in a while. And the preliminary drawings for pasta packaging were not hurrying his step.

"I didn't mean it that way, Oose." He held her hand tightly with the same amber fingers which could crush. "You're worried about your brother. I see why you'd want to force yourself to think about something else."

The white lake is clear and calm. They cannot see it in the massed grey currency of Geneva's business. "I wish he hadn't gone to Cavaglià. He should be here, with Cristina."

"I'm sorry. I didn't realise how much it had affected you."

"Neither did I. It's Brel's fault."

He stopped at a narrow door leading through to a courtyard, and squeezed her hand a little more firmly. "Yes, it is."

"He said that most of the words we use are black and white, and then, from time to time, we use one that's in colour. Those colour words are a part of ourselves, because we give them meaning."

"But only the meaning we want them to have." He released her hand and bent to kiss her on each cheek as softly and intricately as he could. "Why don't you stay here and go shopping? Even if there's nothing you like, it would be better than being stuck alone and in silence in Evian."

"I like Evian," she replied. She didn't say that she liked silence and disliked Geneva. The thoughts were enough. As to solitude, she was not sure. In the car she wound down the window and smoked, singing gently to herself to pass the moments at the border, before

119

the edge of the lake reappeared. "I don't know what time this sad train leaves for Amsterdam."

While they watched the film Fabrice wandered around the strangled, colourless rooms of the cinema. He checked the toilets for latecomers or strays, wound twice up and down the stairs to the projection room for security and slipped quickly outside through the rain to make sure the fire doors were clear. Lucy was usually with him. He hadn't seen the film. Strangely, he didn't want to. Some films, not many, simply didn't raise his curiosity. And Lucy was inside with Alain. Let her, let them, for once.

The foyer was quiet and wide without her. The pale patterned carpet carried its wear marks like heartbeats, deep pink and brown breaths in the crimson. He unlocked the ticket office and sat in the second chair, locking the door behind him. Cashing up would take longer on his own. He looked up at the clock, just over an hour to run, and was grateful for the occupation.

Counting the change he thought of Lucien, saw him still in his ending at his parents' house with his rarer books, his holiday brochures and his fathers' scorn. Had he read the book? Certainly he must have had a copy at the shop, most likely four or five in different languages since the film had been made. There must be a demand for it amongst the tourists looking for light refreshments in the pavement cafés.

Cents built into euros, a separate pile for Swiss francs. He organised a float for the next day, the next showing, replenished the supply of paper tickets. The film would be ending soon, a last chance to grasp at the air outside before the stultified smog of the auditorium, a room of individual odours and collected sighs. He left the office and crossed to the steel and glass of the front doors, opening them to the fresh scent of the rain, a nearing conclusion. The lake was cold and dark. He would see it later.

16
Manitoba III

Jean stopped at Domodossola on the way back, to see if she was there. He asked for the same hotel room, comfort or otherwise in the known, but the room had been allocated, taken. He was given a swipe card for a room on the first floor, looking out at the fashion store and banks. On his way from the reception desk he saw the leaflet bearing Richard's font, or what looked like it. In his suitcase, still packed for Tangiers, Senegal and beyond, was his own copy of the leaflet. Its inks made him long for home. Its text brought other thoughts, the font, permissions. She was not in the hotel.

In Cavaglià Gianluca had been friendlier than before, more open and reactive away from the cognac moments at the restaurant. The memories of the money were forgotten or ignored. In the angled light and long, narrow rooms they chatted like any other father and son, miscommunicating and protective of their own. To the inevitable question of their early return Jean said only that Richard was not speaking, that it was Cristina's decision, that the trip had been long enough and tiring.

"She is a strong woman," Gianluca replied. "Perhaps too strong. I made her that way."

Sophia had been busy in the kitchen, struggling to maintain her maternity in the empty house. She brought them coffee and stayed to hear her husband's declaration. "Yes, you did, Luca. Your work made us all strong."

So this is how we are, Jean thought. We are all amiable enough to suggest, even Cristina, but never to confirm. We trace around the figures on Gianluca's easel with our fingertips. The content is known and unvoiced.

He passed time in their house with the distractions of etiquette, spent the next day away from the thin house to allow Gianluca to create. Alone in Cavaglià he saw the churches and the factories, reined in his walking to feel her childhood hiding in the cold, quiet streets. By chance he found the river, saw snow being led away from the Alps and down to the sea.

The girl at the reception desk was not the same one as on his outward journey. She wore an identical black shirt, loose at the shoulders and fitted at the waist, held her pen in her left hand while she typed, its nib pointing to the ceiling or beyond. The lobby was quiet. Jean-Luc had arrived earlier than he expected to and the hotel's other guests were out for the day. He missed Richard, knew that if he had gone to school he would be home soon, sitting at the kitchen table with his mother and explaining his day, letters shaping in his mind and translating into noises, words, imperfectly formed but improving.

The town was smaller than he had thought. Trains stopped and departed. He walked back through to the wider streets, knowing the route, took a seat next to the doorway of a café to watch the town. Nearby was a shop selling mountain clothing to the few tourists lingering, a morning's late skiing already completed. There were no clear scents to notice, no gardenias or peonies, not even the smell of the milk from the cappuccino brought to him.

Lucy has put her boots on to walk up to her brother's house. On the edge of Evian there are reminders of the rain, trickles of water running from the sodden, sloping ground. The ditches by the side of the road carry soft, resonating flows down towards the lake. It is a day for being quiet and invisible. She is wearing her darkest trousers and a moss-brown jacket, has to step along the tarmac to make herself more noticeable to the traffic. Sentences come to her like sound, fully-formed, loose. The trees are talking to each other. She wonders whether Fabrice still thinks of them.

The road begins to slope downwards as she nears Jean-Luc's house, a consequence of her decision to avoid the centre of Evian and take the wide route, up beyond the old spa and the hospital. Her short hair has grown longer. Small, cold tingles of sweat burst from the heat of her head. She feels her toes push against the toes of her boots and knows that she is almost there. At last the low, high hills are clear of snow. Months of anticipating its arrival are followed each year by waiting for it to leave, even from those dark, stilted spaces in the woods.

Why had Cristina left Domodossola? Luc watched the imitation chocolate dissolve into the milk. Perhaps she had no more to say, or wanted to say it elsewhere. Why had he ordered a cappuccino when he prefers his coffee black, almost always?

She is early or late, it seems. As soon as Cristina opens the door Lucy can tell she is not expected.

"Lunch, yes," Cristina says, leading the way into the kitchen. She puts a frozen pizza in the oven, hearing accusations of cultural treachery, and stands at the corner of the cabinets. "I don't like this kitchen. I don't know why I wanted it this way. It doesn't suit me."

"I think it does." Lucy is standing beside her, with her, watching frail steam looping from the oven's vents and listening to the fan roaring indignantly. "It's a reflection of you, almost a statement of your personality."

The various handles and interlocked granite and marble counters look back. Neat, silver appliances gleam. The steel arms of knives in a knife block exhale their blindness with menaced intent. She loves the room like she loves Cristina. At the far end the worn family table contradicts all other appearances. Lucy imagines and remembers Richard sitting there, held by his mother until he has finished eating, or silently watching the hair at the back of her neck move as she reads and writes her emails. The drawing of a raccoon lies in front of him, unfinished with fascination.

Cristina sees nothing but the impressions of cheese beginning to melt on top of the pizza. "What does that mean? Please, Lucy, don't accuse me. He will be here tomorrow."

They eat in the kitchen and the lounge. A fire has been built but not lit. Cristina sits on the edge of the sofa, leaning over her plate. It would be easy to assume that she wants to fall forward into conversation, to slide into hidden speech and charge the room with her voice, calling, renouncing.

Lucy sees Jean's wicker chair still waiting by the window, where she left it. If there was sunlight it would be cutting angles through the glass and onto the floor. She thinks of the pot of coffee and the biscuits, her refracted morning spent reading, swivelling gently in the chair. She had bought a hair band especially for the occasion, knowing the length of her hair. The house then was large and free.

She had watched the house grow. When she rented her apartment those years earlier Jean-Luc was unmarried. Lucy had been the first to move, left Luc in the family home with its confines and restrictions. The apartment was too small but all she could afford, and it gave her decisions. A round table or a square one? A wardrobe or a long sofa? Should she rest a television on a cabinet or mount a bracket on the wall to leave a clear flow of air from the balcony? And she loved every delayed moment of those decisions, lived in the quiet, unbroken clatter from the street below in anticipation, slipping, instilling.

The wicker chair rotates, both on its central column and on the wheels on its five feet. Manes is carving a picture of Brahma into teak.

Her apartment is still too small and its quiet has altered. A corner of the balcony is always damp, lies in the shade of the other buildings and their affected angles. The twists and bends she has to make to get into the shower annoy her. There is nowhere to store old clothes.

Past meals and nights live in the fabric and the afternoon voices from other apartments infiltrate her. But it is the silence, more so since her first request for Alain to stay. When he is there the space around them is active, physical. When he is not, the three rooms are stained by his presence. His skin lingers. Sounds flail like ripples of water. The quiet, her quiet, is no longer hers.

She thinks she will drive up to the late season café at the foot of the slopes and talk to Astrid. Behind them the freezer will defrost in slow, quickening heartbeats. Soon Astrid will move back to her summer job, the repeating casino welcome she found the previous year when the café closed during the week. Martine and Beatrice returned for the winter and have already left. Astrid is alone, waiting for the snow to end.

Lucy kisses goodbye. Words pass. Should Cristina speak now, while the plates in her hand prevent her from hugging tightly? Lucy kneels to tie the laces on her boots. A car slows for the downhill corner near the house, its engine note decaying. She will walk back into Evian then drive to the ski runs. She could borrow Cristina's car but she doesn't want to ask.

"Thank you for coming," Cristina says. The car accelerates away from the bend. "Are you working tonight?"

Lucy nods.

"Richard will be sad that he hasn't seen you."

Richard, the offer she had made to take him out after school, a half-promise. "I was going to see Astrid at the café. Do you think he would like to come?"

Domodossola was familiar and remembered. He left the stale memory of his coffee and retraced a route back to the racks of postcards and sunglasses, bought three peaches from the boxes of fruit outside the supermarket. The sky was too warm. Two of the peaches passed through his mouth and throat without seeming to produce a sensation of taste. He knew he had eaten them because he had their stones in his hand. He could feel their rough, dry ovals rubbing against his palm. Had he eaten the peaches? Had he fallen into that state of dislocation where everything is seen and heard but nothing is experienced? He was tired, certainly. Colours bled from his senses like words in another language.

There were voices to be heard. He stood on the southbound platform and let a train to Rome come and go. Where had his urgency gone, the energy of flight? The town was familiar. You wonder if he could also recall the smell of inks, recognise the yellow shade of headache as a special offer leaflet ran through the machinery at

124

his command. Would you know that scent, marooned in an Italian afternoon, the temptation of her love?

He tumbled back to the hotel, his room on the first floor, and closed the curtains. Hunger was a false memory. He took off his shoes to sleep, a long, uncomfortable sleep even though it was only quarter past six. The restaurants would fill with faces and sound. He would save the last peach for Richard.

The roundabouts west of Evian are tidy, kept. Ribbons of colour are emerging in planned flowers, words spelt out or images created. As she drives past the supermarket at Amphion Lucy feels closer. She has another twenty minutes until she has to collect Richard from school, turns away from the road and down to the park at the edge of the lake. Two men are walking dogs. A woman is showing her daughter how to throw food to the birds.

She walks away from them to the rocks, an old, stone quay which has crumbled with the winters and inattention since its rectangular replacement took up a concrete position sixty metres nearer to town. She can hear the stowed sailboat tapping at its rubber moorings when she is out over the water. Small catfish flit under her shadow, learning the chance of food. There are no crabs obvious in the wet rocks but she is sure that she could lure them out with a string of chicken skin.

Where she can, away from Cristina's borrowed car and before Richard, she lights a cigarette. The toxins soothe her and reflect, smoke rests in her nose. The lake is a quiet recaptured. She hears the dogs' feet, bread scattering, the low, sonorous repeat of the boat's hull.

Some of the roundabouts have a sponsor's board on them, making you question the impartiality of their message. 'Amphion', says one, or 'Au Bord du Lac', and you wonder what need the Chamber of Commerce and the Hôtel du Savoie have to display such phrases. The colours too, who chooses them? Or are they decided horticulturally by which flowers and shades will bloom together? When these blooms die away will the message stay the same or do the Casino and Tourist Office have other things to say?

Martine and Beatrice have flown back to their summers and Astrid is alone. She has turned half of the chairs upside down and is scrubbing their feet, the bottom of their legs. Richard is happy, he has the treat of a slice of cake and Lucy. His father has collected his car from Cavaglià.

"How's Alain? I haven't seen him for a while."

Lucy rests her hand against her can of Sprite. Its cold, wet metal makes blood rush away from the surface of her skin. She looks down at Astrid's hair and sees the last of her lighter, blonder colours shifting from side to side as she cleans. The strip light and spot lights move the tones as soon as she sees them. Motion brings them and takes them away.

"I like it here in the spring," she says.

Richard has dropped his fork. On the floor by his feet a stain of lime marks the points of impact, a hollow green smear like rust or gold. "Yoose," he cries limply, practising language. Lucy takes another fork from the tray on the counter and passes it to him. She believes Alain, with her café silence.

He calls 'I love you' at unprotected moments and she believes him. Astrid's hair flutters near the bottom of an upturned chair like a wish you once held and have almost forgotten, the kind which leaps back to tempt and tease you moments before sleep. You lie on your side with your hand under the pillow. The room is warm, or the room is cold and your bed is warm. The memory makes you smile before you recognise it, like love.

The hills and mountains are high and the sun sets early and rapidly, switching from calm to a quickening chill. If there is wind it stops being refreshing. Richard runs inside when Lucy returns him and the car. In spite of the breaking of sticks and his learnt consciousness he wants to escape from the long, slow evening, light blue tracing to black as the sun descends on reflective, flatter lands.

Hours can pass as you wait for the day to end and the night to begin. Lucy has the comfort of old shoes to accompany her down the slope to Evian. She will go home and change her socks before work. The roads are still carrying water and smells of resting growth come from the bracken under the trees. The walk is supportive and clean. She feels the muscles above her knees pull and strain, her calves struggle with lactic acid on the steeper sections nearest the town.

She will be late for work, she knows, and will not have time to eat. In the temporary light of her building's entrance hall she sees that flicks of mud have penetrated the bottom of her jeans. In her bathroom mirror she checks her appearance and sees the residue of the day, still out of breath from rushing up to her apartment.

A rare queue has formed outside the cinema. It is the final screening of the film she and Alain saw, she realises. The language of food is unforgotten, stays with her as she walks to work like another voice, mumbling to be heard, until she sees Philippe through the

126

steel and glass doors. His failing hair flaps as he looks from side to side, searching.

"Hurry up, there's so much to do," he says, the closest he can get to admonishment. "Fabrice isn't here. Hurry, please." He locks the door again behind Lucy, his pale blue shirt stretched more tightly than ever over his stomach. As he turns Lucy sees flesh and hair between the buttons.

"Why not? Where is he?"

"I don't know. Get the ticket office ready. I'll be back to hold the doors." He rustles away towards the thin stairs to turn the lights and heating on in the auditorium, throwing the keys towards Lucy. They chime as they land near her feet, claiming haste.

The carpet is cold and fading. As she retrieves the keys her fingers brush the cruel, industrial fibres and she imagines Alain's face, the stubble which would be breaking through the skin of his jaw by that time of day, the almost-black of his eyes. She hadn't enjoyed watching the film. The queue is blocking the dark from coming in. The roundabouts are showing their flowered words and pictures.

Fabrice arrives before Philippe returns. Lucy unlocks the door for him and the viewers who will follow, smiles to say hello, you're late and so are we, the film is supposed to start in ten minutes and there are a lot to get in. Philippe is upstairs. He'll try to be angry but it's all right, you're here now. Can you make sure they come slowly? We need to waste a few minutes until everything's ready or they'll complain. The office is open. Here, hold the door.

A single smile. She waits for him to reach out his arm and block the entrance, then walks across the carpet and into the ticket office. From her chair behind the perforated glass she nods to him and he lets the first few pass. He has tied his scarf in a different way, she notices, and it is new, as black and orange as a cab, although she doesn't know that.

Philippe returns and vanishes again with relief. His shirt is stretched. The queue moves through the foyer and on to the auditorium doors, still locked. When the stream slows Fabrice moves too, takes the keys from Lucy and tears the tickets of the expectant, amiable crowd. Within twenty minutes the loud pre-film advertisements have begun and the cinema is quiet, not full, and complete.

"What happened?" Lucy asks. The toilets are empty. No one is hiding on the thin stairs. The emergency exits are unlocked and free from obstruction.

"I finished."

Lucy doesn't have to ask. She knows what he is talking about. "You've finished?"

He nods.

"It's done?"

"Yes."

Three teenage girls bustle through the front doors, letting them crash behind them. "Are we too late?" one asks.

"No," Lucy answers. She re-enters the ticket office and stands to serve them.

"Is it full?" a second girl asks.

"No."

"Have we missed a lot of the film?" The last girl steps between the others and leans on the glass. Her hair is short, blonde, prances with none of Astrid's unconscious light.

"It's just about to start. Three?" Lucy takes their collected money and tears their tickets. "Be quick," she says, watching Fabrice seeing them through the doors into the auditorium.

His face is still abstracted when he comes back. "The last pages came out of the printer this afternoon. I put them with the others, face down, and just sat there, staring at the whiteness of the pile. When I looked up I was already late. Sorry."

She smiles a wide response. "I was late too, but it doesn't matter, not today. Congratulations. You must be so happy." She moves to hug him.

He shrugs, his arms by his sides. "I didn't realise how close to the end I was. I thought I still had a few weeks to go. And then it was all there, stacked in plain, white sheets." He pauses, at last takes his scarf off in the warming foyer. "I went to visit my grandmother a couple of days ago. I didn't know what to say to her."

The scarf hangs from his hand like a garland. Below it the pale reds and pinks of the paling carpet seep their brutal roughness. "Shall we sort out the money now, or do you want to go outside for a while first? The wind's gone and it's a clear night. Cold, but clear."

Jean-Luc has not seen his bedroom for over three weeks. He wonders what it will smell and taste of, how the warming air will have changed it, how he will feel when he sees its whites and creams.

17
Evian V

The pillows were pillow-shaped. There were no dents in them, no impressions of where she lay. Normally their bed was half-made, pillows and duvet thrown carelessly and easily into an approximation of where they should be. Luc wondered what he should do with the dirty clothes in his suitcase, carried them into their bathroom to find that the lid was closed on the lined, wicker basket.

Was this a message from her, or another example of this strange, perfect neatness? The mirrored doors on the medicine cupboard were slid shut. Her body lotions, cleanser, toner and night cream were in a line by the sink. Two almost-full bottles of shampoo and conditioner were at the corner of the bath. He flicked the lid of the laundry basket open with his foot and dropped his clothes onto hers, then took them out again.

Sunday, the quiet reverie after the last showing. Lucy indulges the morning in her shorts and nightshirt. When the sunlight reaches all but the damp corner of her balcony she will open the doors, has arranged to meet Alain for a slow lunch to substitute for the long family tradition of long family lunches. Afterwards they will walk by the lake or in one of the parks, perhaps drive over to Châtel and watch the walkers descend on the pâtisseries and gift shops.

He will put his arm around her, you think, walk in stride with her, his free hand pushed into the pocket of a black coat, hip-length, collar half up, well-made and functional. His coat, his almost black hair, his skin, the hidden message of his fierce eyes. You know him, can hear gentility in his troubadour voice, see the shapes of affection in the lines around his mouth.

And Lucy will be with him, interpreting, wondering whether he will eat the risotto and lamb shanks she is planning on cooking for them both, and if so would he still have preferred tomatoes, oil and yoghurt?

Will his shoulders look beautiful in the late light of the apartment, and again later, as she looks down to see his arms reaching around her waist? When they are asleep will the silence of the apartment rest into itself?

Until then she has the morning and her shorts and nightshirt. She wears a hair band and reads Stendhal, listens to the street below her balcony with a packet of biscuits by her side and good coffee.

Somewhere she wishes she had Jean's rotating chair and the high, angled window, another language.

For the first day Luc dealt with the matter-of-fact, the concrete, the exact. Once he had finished unpacking and put his clothes in the washing machine he opened his mail and looked over the house for signs of their absence, then spent an hour calling and emailing to cancel the bookings for the rest of their trip. When Christina brought Richard home from school the afternoon was lost to play and tales, mostly in the security of his bedroom. They stayed up late together, so late that once Richard had heard most of a story and fallen asleep it was too late to begin another conversation.

Cristina was quiet, as quiet as you would expect. They circled around each other. Rooms were claimed for the evening and then abandoned. Jean-Luc's immediate, enduring concern was answered when she paused at the foot of the stairs, near the door to the lounge.

"I'm going to bed. Will you come up soon?"

He looked past her to the fast-aging beech of the staircase. So he could share her bed, their bed. Indeed, he was expected to. How long should he wait before joining her?

The heaviness of the drive and arrival came to him. The hours with Richard had been happy, the chance to chatter in their secret way, but even then the house around them had been home to a lurking, imaginative lull. The sofa was comfortable. There were two other bedrooms he could use. He had looked in both of them earlier to see if their beds were made, just in case.

How long? Calculations came to him as automatically as those for a print run, numbers of colours and copies, trims, folds, stapling or other finishes. She would wash, brush her teeth. There were treatments to apply, clarifying lotion and night eye tincture. She would probably tie her hair up. At least ten minutes, fifteen to be sure, anything to avoid the complication of seeing her naked as she changed.

"Have you heard from Jean-Luc or Cristina?" Alain asks.

In her sleep Lucy is at the airport, listening to the reverse thrust of an Airbus arriving from Stockholm. She knows it has come from there because the public address system has just announced it, and she can see the logo on the tailfin as the plane taxis in. She is sitting in the café, resting her head against the window. The cold of the glass filters through her hair to the back of her neck. A short, dark man in a black shirt brings her a thick paper cup, says "Sorry for the delay," and lays a wooden stirrer and two colours of sugar on the table.

130

The drink is tea, light and pale. It has no milk in it. Beside her is a folded newspaper. She knows every story, can recite them in columns if you want her to. Apart from the man in the black shirt, clearing tables to her left, she is alone. The terminal is quiet. Desks are empty and closed and the morning deliveries have not yet begun to appear. A woman in the familiar uniform of a car rental company walks past. She had taken her shoes off as soon as she locked her kiosk and she slides across the cleaned floor in stockinged feet. Lucy hears them swish in the blossoming silence.

Next to her, around her, Alain stumbles naked through his sleep. The skin of his stomach glimmers in the almost dark as town light penetrates the edges and joins of the curtains.

Her apartment does not have space for him. It is hers, a possession. She clears herself away before he comes, makes room for his speech and movement, but every sentence is filled with her choices, her negotiations of furniture or design. The angle of the clock is hers. She keeps loose coins in a white bowl on the table. The curtains at the balcony doors are yellow and yellowed. They do not quite reach the floor. He loves her, has claimed to the lake that she is more real than he. Love, passion, more real than any you can imagine, as proud and insistent as the tail lights of the ferry shouting its arrival in Lausanne. He would swim across the water to her if he could.

His skin glimmers. You hear him say Lucy, Lucie, Oose, wondering at the instance of his language. You think you see a shimmer in his eyes but you are wrong, he is looking away to keep you from believing you are being inspected. The apartment has no space for him and he is there, sleeping with his love, his lover. Memories fly like cries and whispers.

Maman Sulpice wrote letters. From the neatly arranged lines of replies you would guess she wrote hundreds, perhaps thousands. There were the obvious ones, of course, her brother still in Dijon, her sister, chased to the warmth of a village somewhere near Perpignan. Her children too, a son and his wife and child in Besançon, seemingly stuck in charge of a branch of the prison service, and Fabrice's father.

The letters back from Dijon were the most natural, the easiest to decode. To begin with Fabrice resisted them. He left them at Maman Sulpice's house while her inheritors decided what to do with it, negotiating and revising their ideals. Her nephews wanted to keep it as an escape by the water. Her eldest son saw its sale as retirement. Fabrice's father asked him to check on the light rooms and wooden floors once a week, wanted reports on the state of the garden. Fabrice did as he was requested. The letters and books were his on her precise statement, duly attested and signed. He had begun to collect boxes for their inevitable removal.

He read the first letter, a register of occurrences, as rain trapped him inside. Maman Sulpice had willed it so. He was curious. It was from his father, described life in Dijon as it was then, the places she knew which had changed, incidents and actions. His own name was mentioned twice although he couldn't recall the moments so carefully catalogued. The voice was clear, spoke in the structured, erudite manner of a child trying to be honest or well taught. Fabrice recognised the handwriting, at least.

Slowly the boxes were filled and carried over to his apartment. The family letters were mostly comfortable, reminiscences of distant cousins, proud aunts proclaiming the virtue of their offspring. And it was aunts, he noticed, daughters and nieces. The few from male relations, for it was only a few, were lined with formality. Birthday presents received. Notes which had evidently accompanied invitations, lost or stored elsewhere. Letters of duty, of consolation. Holiday accounts. Details of visits to Evian, arrivals, intentions.

The female letters, for those pages were surely as female as their authors, seemed to Fabrice to be extensions of conversations. Yes, he read information he did not know, sometimes private, physical information, but it was as if the aunts, daughters and nieces had wanted to tell their stories face to face instead of on the telephone.

Paper sufficed. Its readers heard the words in a different place on a different day, away from the judgement of breathing, listening. It was the closest they could come to eye contact. Messages were passed on. Lives, if not quite shared, were connected.

The second day was like the first. At night Jean wants to clutch her to him, not from possession or desperation but with longing. Wind shuffles the trees of their woods, their leaves, their broken sticks.

Akash sleeps in a cot in his parents' bedroom, close enough for Manjusha to reach out and touch him. Most nights end with him caught between her and Manes, his legs curled and his face close to the reckoning of her chest. The girls share the only other bed and bedroom, lie sometimes at each end and sometimes side by side. They are Swiss in everything but history, have grown to treat the Nepali they speak at home as a consequence rather than an origin. French words mingle and interject. They think mostly in French. Manjusha worries that her daughters will not recognise Darjeeling when they go, as she is sure they will.

Carvings are building up like lines of writing stacked against the wall. There are so many off-cuts of wood resting in rows in the bedroom that she is finding it difficult to slide open the wardrobe door and put his work clothes away. She will ask him to move them closer together, or store new ones somewhere else. She doesn't know where.

Fabrice had already read the most recent letters. Before she died he would collect the mail from her house, redirect those with a typed address to his father then carry the rest to her hospital room. He offered to write replies for her, to let her dictate and hear back her words before returning with a neat copy for her to sign.

"Words flow when you write them yourself. It's not the same process when you say them out loud. You should know that, Doudou."

"But won't they be worried if they don't get an answer?"

"Only if they do not know me. And if so then I don't want to hear from them. Read me another one. Are there any more?"

He read, eventually. Before she would let him open each letter he had to describe it, the colour of the envelope, its shape and size, the weave of the paper, a watermark. Next he had to comment on the stamp, its placing and origin, explain how her name and address had been written. Was it 'Madame Sulpice' or 'Amantine'? Did the lettering slope forwards or backwards? Was the address offset or in a line? Was there a return address on the back, and if so, describe its appearance without reading it out?

"Isabelle," she would say at last, "Madame Leiris," or "Hélène," then close her eyes and settle into her pillows as if deciding what she was to hear.

As he flicked through those letters again Fabrice studied their envelopes. He wanted to know what she had learned from them, how she would calculate and quantify, give more attention to his voice once she had considered that of their authors. There was no need to reread those letters themselves, no impetus. Their contents were her death and its approach. She was a figure on a bed defined by the shapes she made in the covers, a blind over the window, reflections of light making their uneasy way through her eyes. The images which came from her mind, the definitions of herself still spoken, rarely corresponded to his understanding of her.

"Remember how to sleep, Doudou. It's easy to sleep." She was an ending.

Alain is sleeping with his love, his lover. When they wake together she will let him use the shower before she gets out of bed.

In the early mornings Geneva is forty-five kilometres and an hour away, sometimes more.

Coffee, of course, ubiquitous and contemplative. She will lay out some breakfast for him, mix yesterday's bread with supermarket cheeses and jams, perhaps warm a couple of pastries as he dries himself. The gentle sweetness of last night's risotto will wait in the air like a memento.

His car is in the garage beneath his apartment. When he leaves she will readjust and recalculate, clear the table or eat slices of bread before or after her shower. Her hair might seem longer, still lacking elegance or fluidity. The pores around her eyes might be closed and loose like a bruised apple. Her fingers might read a new version of the contours of her waist, the force of his arms around it. He will drive to work with the heater on and thoughts of her. At Amphion the traffic will already be queuing at the roundabouts.

The other replies, the unfamilial and unknown, were more intriguing. Letters had been sent from across Switzerland and Italy, from Prague, Missouri and North Carolina, from Malta. Half of a whole shelf was taken up by correspondence from New Zealand, each identical envelope slotted in chronologically like pages of a great novel. As Fabrice lifted them into a box to take to his apartment he saw that the rest of the shelf, and some of the one below, held letters from Dijon in the same handwriting. He took those too. That was enough for that visit. They would last him.

He settled into hearing the voice of Amantine's friend. Amantine, always Amantine. She had begun to write even before Maman Sulpice had moved to Evian, small notes of thoughts, continuations of discussions they had shared. As the women aged the letters grew longer, told of preparations for New Zealand and the life discovered there. Sometimes Fabrice suspected personal details approaching and skipped ahead until he thought it was safe to return. Other times he found himself suddenly immersed in gall bladder operations, gynaecology and others' grounds for divorce, and he would hurry away from such invasions with surprised guilt.

Quickly he began to feel as though he had been shown a previously hidden method of speaking, one in which he had not been told the rules of language. The experience starved him. All that remained was the sensation that he was holding a telephone away from his ear and was only able to hear every other word. Nothing he could do would bring the receiver closer.

In other rooms in other houses there would be Maman Sulpice's replies, a conversation. He would never know how she spoke. The thought made him infinitely sad, so sad that he put away the final, questioning letters from New Zealand and turned instead to the racks of other letters, leaving them unread. And they each had an envelope to decipher, a task he could do without the curse of their half-spoken contents.

On the third day, Monday, Cristina took Richard to school after his joyful weekend, the gift of unresolved, unbroken time with his father still carrying him into the new week.

"Lamp," he had said the night before, after stories and kisses. Not amp, yamp or hamp, but lamp, so plainly that Luc had asked him to repeat it. "Lamp," he said again.

"That's right, lamp. Well done." Luc kissed him again, then kissed his raccoon, as usual. Nothing was different. If he had spoken out or celebrated the child might have become self-conscious. He didn't even tell Cristina, in case it wasn't true.

The airport is filling up as the morning urgency takes hold. As he leaves the terminal at the end of his shift Manes thinks about saying good morning to a customs officer he recognises. The man walks quickly towards him, towards the doors, strides so purposefully that Manes decides he must be late and lets him pass unhindered.

The apartment will be empty when he gets home, he knows. The girls will be on their way to school. He might even see them at the bus stop, getting on as he gets off. Manjusha will have taken Akash to the shops or to a friend's house so that he can sleep. She will wake him for a late lunch, prepare breakfast and light, clear tea without milk for him. They will talk and smile, and Akash will play.

Yes, the apartment is empty. Manjusha has gone out in spite of the letter for Manes. She didn't need to stay to see him open it because she knows what it will say, does say. Finally, and on time, his father is dead. She is tall, not quite too tall. Her body has learnt how to carry itself. It swims and sways. Her skin will welcome the warm, wet embrace.

18

Cavaglia IV

"It must have started in Cavaglià, when Luca left. Or before that, in the months when the house was so full of noise that Papa couldn't begin to work. 'Il Linguatore', they call him now. Did you know that?"

"Yes," Jean mumbles, not wanting to interrupt her with sounds or silence.

"'Il Linguatore', 'The Maker of Words'. He lets them, of course. He likes the title, thinks it justifies the time he spends crafting, and that unspeakable quiet." She pauses, considering implications and sidelines. "Why do they matter, those black designs? Why are they so important that we had to feel our way along the walls in case the crack of a light switch moved his hand?"

"Richard," Jean says.

"Yes, Richard." They are in the cavern of the café. Lucy's visit to talk to Astrid has brought it back to Cristina's memory.

As soon as she returned from taking Richard to school she began to speak. Light colours at first, creams and yellows of routine actions, shopping, cleaning, preparing. Luc answered her questions. He made statements and suggestions, obeying her display. In the reflecting stare of the kitchen she moved slowly to browns and greens, saying "Richard missed you" as easily as she could, and with the softest shades of new growth, "Where did you go?"

It was her idea that they should go out, away from the house. She drove them to the café with the car window open, using the road noise to fill her obvious, clustered space. Jean bought them both drinks to excuse their presence. Cristina rested her elbows on the table and her chin on the back of both hands. She breathed in and closed her eyes until the sound came.

"I saw the font on a leaflet for a glacier trip," Jean-Luc says. "Or I think I did. I brought one back to show you. It's at home."

"They were one of the first to ask, the tourist board for the Italian Alps. I suppose they must have already heard of Papa's work."

"So you said they could use it?"

"Yes. It would have been difficult to say no. And it seemed right."

"I didn't know. I don't think you told me."

Cristina's head is bowed forward. Her gaze is directed at the table between them, the physical space. He has sat across from me, she thinks, her eyes not seeing. She sips from her hot chocolate, the fingers of both hands holding on to the edge of the cup. Words lead themselves slowly through blue to red, as they must.

"When Luca left." She lowers the cup and rests it delicately on its saucer. The sounds of contact are as natural as love. "Before he left my mother and I became even quieter. We'd limp around the house, moving from room to room only if we had to. We spoke gently, not excessively, manufactured a kind of shorthand language. Sometimes she would say whole sentences with the shapes of her eyes or hands.

"Don't misunderstand me, Jean-Luc. You've met her, you know how she is. I'm not trying to bargain for her, to say she sacrificed herself. She was happy, perhaps happier then than she is now. She had her family around her, living, being, talking. The house ran to rhythms and motions she created, not Papa. He worked because she let him."

Jean nods to show he has heard, to imply he has understood. He is looking at her, seeing the tips of her fingers still holding her cup. He sees too the marks on her back from the skiing accident and wants to hold her, softly, for a long time. He nods. She has to speak. He has to listen.

"But it was almost as if we were compensating for Luca, reducing ourselves to keep an equilibrium. It didn't work." She shifts her left hand away from his glare and onto her leg, scratches the harsh cotton of her jeans. The noise of her nails disturbs her. "Luca got louder, then he left. I'm glad he did because he had to, for himself, but it altered everything, spoiled it perhaps. 'Il Linguatore'. He didn't write for years, not well, not until Richard."

She stops for him, waits for his response. "Look at me, please."

He looks. "What are you saying? Because of Luca? Because of Richard?"

"No, Jean, because of me. Because of nothing."

"Because of nothing."

"Yes." She brings her hand back up towards the cup and almost reaches out for him. The colours in her eyes are shaking endlessly through crimson and blood to black. "There's nothing, darling, don't you see? Quiet, that silence. This is how I am." The worn wood of the table glimmers up at her. A pale shine, a reminder. Her voice is soft and slow, like a leaf growing or falling, like a lover's. "I speak in broken silence and no one can hear me. I love Luca, I love my mother and father, and I love you. I want to go to the top of Cornebois and watch you ski down, then call out that love in a hundred different voices and rush towards you."

The cup rattles in its saucer, sounds of contact. Cristina watches it fall still. "Don't you see, Jean? Can't you hear it?"

What is she saying in the cool spring café, while Astrid prepares for the season's ending and trails of water begin to dry up on the greening hills? There are three other cars in the car park, Astrid's small, local Renault and those of walkers scaling to the tree line. Their bright coats and spilling breaths are visible from the café windows. In Evian the town is being itself, listing in the boughs of the lower mountains. Beside it the lake waits for its moment to speak.

Cristina says 'love' and 'nothing', as if to explain all she can. You know she is still talking as she sits there, offering information in other forms and constructions. Those sounds she makes, the vocal twists and complexities, falter in their display. Her languages collude and deny.

Yet 'love' she said, a repercussion. Perhaps she cannot phrase it because it is true, and to project it outwards would simply be to fool you in some way, or at least to give you a part of a whole, a suggestion. She waits instead, anticipating, prejudging your reaction.

'Love' and 'nothing', two attempts to include. For minutes she has no more words, or none spoken, leaves Jean to interpret how he chooses. And it is his choice, as clear and incursive as the rough, dry stone of a peach. He has listened to her, heard the details of that mythological house where Gianluca drew Richard's font. For a passing second he sees the tall, graceful curves of the upstrokes and the wide capitals, imagines the importance of the messages it describes. The café window lets him see the yellow coat of a walker between the high firs. He could choose love.

He could choose love, could process his knowledge and his memory into the urge to look at the strobes of her lowered eyes and hold her. His understanding of her is different from yours, comes from the accumulation of imagined moments you could not have seen. The version of Cristina he reasons himself to, his composition, allows him to love. It encourages him, it enraptures him, precisely because that is the outcome he wants. He could be mistaken, but you are not him. He has love or nothing, her nothing.

She raises her gaze to try to see an impression of his thoughts, decides to speak again. "Lucy came for lunch a few days ago. She was talking about Alain, about how he can't understand her when she talks about passion. Can't, or won't try to. 'Sometimes we use a word that's in colour', she said, 'and those words in colour are a part of ourselves, because we give them meaning.'"

"That's a strange thing for her to say."

"She didn't. She did, but she was repeating Brel."

"She likes Brel."

The table draws their voices down again. Quiet hums come from the strip lights in the display cabinets and the temperature regulator of the freezer forces a new rumble of pumped fluid. Jean-Luc has to listen.

"She said that Alain talks about love, tells her he loves her, but doesn't want to hear her when she tries to mention passion."

Love, and nothing.

"And you, what do you want to talk about?" Luc asks. The yellow coat of the walker is out of sight and he feels the wanted strike of a violet headache. He is sleepy and awake, more revived by her presence with him than he is ready to show. "Why are we here, Cristina? Why this place, this café?"

Astrid looks over to their used cups. The freezer warbles indifference.

Cristina pauses, balancing. "We first met him here, all of us."

The radio on the shelf responds to Astrid's stretching hand. She will see Lucy, be able to tell her that she chose not to be able to hear what was being said. Her hair tangos in gold and blonde in the nearby spotlight.

"There's nothing," Cristina says.

Jean lifts his fingers from the table as if to point or reach. He slides his palm towards her, a fragment of appeal in his raised fingertips. "Tell me. Tell me now, while we're here."

"I don't know how to explain it."

"Try," he says, barely audibly. "Please."

"There's nothing," she repeats, "There never was. I wanted, I still want, to speak, to be heard at last. It was me, Jean-Luc, always. I am someone else."

"I don't understand."

She is wearing her second-best jeans, short shirt and blue jacket, the clothes he imagined. Her feet are crossed, gripping on to themselves under her chair. She squeezes her knees together for energy and determination then sits up and back. Her hands are still clutched on the table, waiting. Her hair has fallen from behind her ears.

"In the restaurant at Cavaglià I was Cristina, Il Linguatore's daughter. Richard nearly slept against my arm, do you remember? I heard Italian on the trains and at the airport, my language. It didn't sound like me." She glances at the radio, almost seeing the noise coming from it. "I don't want to be silent, Jean-Luc. I want to be someone to swim with. Not for, but with. I love. I need to say it."

"Then say it."

"I can't," she says softly, then again, louder, "I can't," then again, louder, attacking the hard consonants, "I can't." She pushes out her hands at her cup and it rattles from its saucer and onto its side. A brown stream runs out like a sentence or a sound, spilling.

She calms. Astrid lifts her head from the storage racks under the counter, her selected chore of organisation. She sees the couple and the spreading chocolate, and returns to her task. Cristina calms.

"I can't, Luc. Please, darling, try to hear me. There's nothing to say except that I love you and I can't say it out loud, not in the ways I want to. Let's ski again, let's swim, let's talk about passion. Let's be still in our own house, you reading in your wicker chair and me on the sofa, creating our own silence instead of allowing one to come to us."

19
Geneva IV

The letters from the United States intrigued him. It appeared that Americans had a different way of writing addresses. The lines were staggered ever so slightly across, as if the hands which had written them had wanted to set them evenly, the French way, but needed always to see the first letter of the line above to make certain they were in the correct position.

In doing so they were naturally misaligned, yet Fabrice was pleased by the consistency of their offset placements. He liked the way those hands had always put the final line, 'France', in capitals, as if to emphasise how far each envelope had to travel. How many letters were sent overseas from the United States, he wondered? Was there a percentage known, or was the total so small that it was unworthy of computation?

Perhaps those capital letters were a reflection of the difference, a statement to be noticed. And every envelope was written in blue ink, with a return address in the top left corner, uniform and regulated. They were accurate and efficient, like their stamps. He had a compulsion to ignore their broken seals and tear them open to see whether the details of lives inside were equally well arranged, or whether the letters' contents hid randomly behind the show of order. But the New Zealand conversations still clung to him, the relentless distance of the missing voices. He settled for lining up the envelopes in chronological rows to watch their handwriting change over time.

There is a queue at the ticket office, six people in three pairs. It is enough to keep Alain from the glass. Between serving customers Lucy sees his hands. He is stroking the inside of his index finger with his thumbnail, gently running it up and down the skin of the joints like he strokes her arms. In the seconds it takes for one couple to take their tickets, move away and be replaced by the next she can see the tendons pull and release. The motions make her recognise his intent, although she doesn't realise it. When the last of the couples leave she has already formed a response, made unknowingly from the memory of his touch on her forearms. Languages compile themselves and die away, as instantly and automatically as waves on the lake or in the air.

He smiles at her, his lips, teeth and eyes combining to transmit another message. His hands are in the pockets of his coat, she notices.

The couples are inside. Philippe will project the programme, inserting the right advertisements and trailers. The film is old and French, imposed upon the cinema in exchange for the more recent successes. He will not be surprised at the smallness of the takings or the speed with which Fabrice returns from the auditorium doors, says a silent hello to Alain and leans to tap on the glass of the ticket office.

"Is that it?"

"Did you think there would be more?" Lucy replies.

"No, I suppose not." He is in front of the window, blocking Lucy's view. "What do you want to do now? It's two hours long so we've got plenty of time to get everything done."

She looks back at his wide, clear eyes, so much clearer even in the few days since he finished. "We could go outside for a while, if you want, and do this later?" As she makes her suggestion she raises her eyebrows and twitches her head to signify Alain.

"You want a cigarette. That's what you're saying, isn't it?" He smiles happily, free of the trees. "But the sky has a wonderful smell tonight. It's almost vanilla, but there's honey or yeast in it as well, something sweet and colourful."

Most of the letters from North Carolina were in envelopes the colour of fresh yeast, he remembers. Reading them must have placed the reference in his vocabulary. He had watched the regular lines on them begin to slope downwards with age. He pictured the hand growing weaker, saw how the letter n in Amantine and Evian slowly collapsed into being only a squashed, bumpy line. North Carolina in the top left corner became NC. He guessed it was a female hand. He couldn't be sure, not without opening one of the letters, as the return address gave only initials, but when he imagined the fading hand it always seemed female.

It was the same with so many of Maman Sulpice's correspondents. They grew old with her and they died. The last letter from Missouri was in an expensive, white envelope and her address had been typed. He had to study the postmark and printed header to work out what it was. The span of months between it and the previous, final handwritten one, all scrawl and cipher, decided the matter. He was glad he hadn't read any of them.

The far roar and descending lights of a plane are passing Evian on their way to Geneva. "It's the wind," Alain says to Lucie as the tail light moves away. "It's coming along the water from the city."

Lucie looks up at the plane, then at Alain. "I can't feel any wind."

142

"We're sheltered here. But there must be some, or they wouldn't use that runway and approach." She keeps looking at him for an explanation. He knows his eyes are blacker outside, less easy to avoid. He stares straight out, waiting for her to finish smoking, waiting for a moment he is not sure will arrive, but he senses her question and shrugs. "You learn about wind and flight paths very quickly when you work in the centre of Geneva. Some days it's loud, some days it's not."

"Which is better?" she asks, jokingly.

"That depends on what we're doing. If we're supposed to be having design conferences then it needs to be quiet or we have to go somewhere else. If we're working on, for example, crisp packets or biscuit wrappings, then noise is fine. Sometimes it's helpful." He is about to say more, to clarify, when he hears her laughing as quietly as she can.

"Alain," she says. Cigarette smoke hangs near her like a nimbus.

He turns his head to her, sees the side of her nose dancing as she quells her laughs. "My job is important, you know."

"No it's not."

He thinks. "No, you're right. It's not. It's trivial, and probably meaningless. But I'm good at it and it pays well. I was called into a meeting today and told so."

"I'm sorry. You are, and it does." She takes hold of his hand in contrition, his draughtsman's hand, the one which can crush, flex and stroke. If she holds it in her own it will be unable to contain her.

The last of the plane disappears from the reach of their hearing. Spare clouds are whispering in front of the stars and the night is as cold as it is going to be. Perhaps by the morning those clouds will merge and drop, making a sheen of mist over the water. She wraps her fingers around his and watches the surface of the lake move in soft flows.

"When we are at the airport, what do you do?"

The carvings in Manes's apartment line the feet of the walls like icons. Small, irregular rectangles of rosewood and teak have crawled to the short hallway. Stories look out at other stories opposite them.

European envelopes were easy to translate. Their stamps and postmarks gave them away before he could contemplate the words themselves, the curls and flicks of another language, the peculiar spacing of letters from the Czech Republic or the diffident glide of Sorrento. He tried for a while to understand the inflections of the return address in Finland but all he could manage to specify with accuracy was 98100 Kemijärvi. The precise street name and number kept itself hidden, as did the reason for Maman Sulpice's address to be in the simplest, separated characters.

Days after the trees of Manitoba had left him he cleared the last shelf of letters, not seeing them as he packed them into boxes and came accidentally to Canada. In the filling world of his apartment he saw Québec written across the rear, triangular flap of a milk envelope, raw and untreated. It was inscribed in a formal, accustomed hand, black ink, the kind of handwriting which proclaims it has no need for deception or misinformation. A man's handwriting, certainly, although even as he thought it Fabrice knew he would never check to see if he was right.

Who did Maman Sulpice write to in Canada? She had not mentioned anyone, not even in those long, desperate times at her bedside when they had both struggled for words other than her health. Those moments were ideal. It would have been a unifying impulse, a chance at least for them to share an identity, a private notion. But he didn't form a connection, not then with Maman Sulpice, not in his apartment with the presumed man who called her Amantine, and not with his own, unspoken version of Canada.

Instead he concentrated on the official marks on the envelopes, watched with fascination as they migrated over time from English to bilingual to French. It was more than the removal of language. The stamps changed too, became more proud and visible, almost louder. And the handwriting, the sudden inclusion of accents, loops and swirls appearing on numbers.

Somewhere awareness was exerted, styles and spellings examined, clarified, legitimised. Fabrice looked carefully at each envelope, at its mix of old design and new speech. Slowly he felt the thickness of the letters change, not in a way which implied that less or more was being written but rather that the paper itself had altered. Did the change of paper come with a different voice? And the words inside, surely crafted as carefully as those on the outside, ergonomic and particular, were they saying the same things? Would characters look odd and out of place? Perhaps that was why Maman Sulpice had not mentioned him. The explanation would have been too hard for her to convey. Her eyes could only see light, or sometimes the thinner pink of her eyelids when sleep would not come.

Why had she chosen to give her letters to him? The question still persisted, stronger since Fabrice had cleared the last shelf. He had heard her words read out, those special phrases of bequest so closely inspected and reworked after her husband died, a reason as lost as the origin of her blue dress. The books could go to Lucien, all except

144

the George Sand, but he would take care of her letters. They would be his, be her. He didn't know why.

Manjusha is packing their possessions into large, strong boxes. There will not be many when she is finished. The furniture came with the apartment, the crockery and cooking utensils will stay, as will those bedclothes and curtains she cannot give to her friends. Most of the children's clothes will be wanted by others, especially Akash's, although the girls are older, will insist on keeping some of theirs, she's sure.

She doesn't yet know what she will do with the pages of carvings. They may be beautiful and intimate signs of Manes, but they are only practice and play. She will gauge the cost, ask him when he gets home. It is late, too late still to be packing in the sharp light. She is tired and should go to bed. There is so much to do in the morning.

A swathe of men and women, mostly men, are colonising the airport. They wear the names of their employers on their backs of their fluorescent yellow jackets like divisions. Manes has been assigned to a cleaning trolley, as usual. Others have their obliged habits of floor cleaners or collection cages, and they dissipate through the concourses and waiting areas, slow polishing, spraying, wiping, scrubbing, emptying. He has told only his supervisor and the few faces he will pass regularly through the night that it is his last shift. They were not surprised. They come and go.

Clean and move. The terminal processes its last passengers of the day. Kiosks and shops close. Customs officials lock doors. Within two hours the building shines to stillness. A few seats are claimed, figures stretched across their curving edges, heads resting on a coat or a jumper pulled from a suitcase. Clean and move. The stillness is unbroken by the movement of those in yellow jackets.

At the café Manes looks quickly for Lucy, knowing she will not be there. Two newspapers have been left folded on one of the tables and he wonders if she was reading them before he started work. The seats are tea green, he notices, as green as the steppes of Darjeeling. His father is dead.

If he saw Lucy would he speak to her? He is impulsive, he knows that, impulsive enough to marry Manjusha and move to Switzerland. What would he say? And now, returning to India to take up his father's work. He has earned the money he needs, has saved and spent aware that his father would die. There are three people in the café, sharing time to waste at a table. Manes glances at them as he passes by but Lucy is not there.

He cleans, he moves. As the floors are washed and the concourse cleared of bags of rubbish from the check-in desks the building becomes brighter. New angles of light appear, reflections and impressions cast in the empty terminal like remembered ambitions. He nods to acquaintances as they cross, regardless of whose branding they wear, carries out his tasks with the same pragmatic enthusiasm he has always known. It is not until he returns his trolley and jacket that he thinks of the ending, the future.

At the automatic glass doors he sees cabin crew and desk staff arrive, a new, enlarged shift of security guards, one by one. Workers for the shops and restaurants unzip coats as they approach the day. A dark blue and grey morning hesitates outside, lazy and unwilling. Above the doors a line of lights illuminates the paved entrance, hard lights on the canopy as if to prove a welcome. Manes sees their shine in the face of a woman he recognises, the assistant manager of a sandwich bar. Many times she has given him pastries as the store closes rather than throw them away.

"Hello," she says, "done for the night?"

"Yes." Her teeth look bright. The halogen glow is cruel, brutal almost. The image brings the easier colours of north east India to him, the high towns where every shade is made smoother and more gentle. His Switzerland has been understood by those other colours, the sharp snares which echo the city and urge the sky to delay its arrival. He will take his father's work with care, carve intricate patterns into teak and form them into tea caddies for the plantation tourists. But those pictures will be myths and tales, histories, not the images of Mont Blanc and Geneva he has created in his apartment. He has seen the lines beginning to form behind him, waiting for flights. His father's customers may come from those queues.

"Goodbye," he says, and smiles in return. Her pace slows as if she wants to talk, a reason to stay in the clearer air a little while longer, but he nods to confirm his goodbye and walks on. If she was Lucy, and he spoke to her, what would he say?

"What do you mean?"

"While I'm at the café, reading a newspaper, where do you go?"

Alain feels her fingers in his. She is holding them more tightly than usual. "Nowhere." He thinks of the white shutters on the shops, their steel perforations allowing him images of what they protect. The water is dark and invasive, its wide depths looming out for as far as he can see.

"I walk around. It's a different place when it's empty. It's like its purpose has been stolen, or else the construction has just been

146

finished and it's waiting for its grand opening." He pauses, feels the breeze from a late-returning bird move through his vision. "I don't think I like it, but I know you do. If you want to go there tonight, after work, then I'd like to come with you."

Lucie releases herself from his hand and turns to him, away from the lights of Lausanne. "You keep asking me why I never tell you I love you," she says to the full, cruel brown of his eyes. "That's why. Because you say things like that."

"I don't understand."

"I know."

They spin to quiet, her quiet, their eyes looking at each other's for some source of recognition. If you saw them standing at the shore you would think they were lovers, two people so close together and staring without the need to move or look away, like lovers do. You might wonder if a great event was about to be played out, one of those sequences of moments or minutes which you will remember, although the details will change each time you think of it until what you think of as a memory will only be a representation, an imperfect expression. And you have been thinking so carefully about those lovers' moments or minutes that you have not heard Alain ask her to have dinner with him. You have missed the frantic seconds of language when Lucy dragged her teeth at the scar on her bottom lip to feel the numbness.

"Please," Alain says, watching her mouth distort with the unnoticed action. "There's something I want to ask you, to talk to you about, and I don't want to do it here, by the water."

At the corner of the cinema behind them Fabrice has not seen their eyes break contact either. He is looking past them and around them, seeing only that he has spent two tranquil afternoons reading envelopes from Québec, trying to learn their language. He has fallen to lightness, an ease you could only see in the loose smile he carries like a memento. In the brighter reflections of the canopy he has realised that in spite of those Canadian hours he has not thought of Toronto.

20

Amsterdam II

Not one thought, not even when he first saw the nationality of a stamp or the word Canada spelt out in a return address. Fabrice's looseness sees the lake as the calm, clear space between three trees, lost in woodland, clearer. Lucy's water is breathing, waiting in soft flows. To Alain the dark, embedded surface is an obstacle to avoid. Fabrice's lake, from the corner of the cinema, is a loosened clearing. Water and language, images and response.

Cristina has taken off her boots and socks, stretches her legs out on the sofa and rubs her feet against the cool stone fabric. She can hear the sounds of Jean and Richard performing for each other, one booming and squeaking the voices of a story, the other giggling, shouting out recognised choruses.

Richard splashed more in the bath. Bubbles and plastic animals were thrown or dropped onto the floor. They are not restored yet, Luc and Cristina, but Richard is happy and Jean-Luc is home. For the moment that is enough for her. Perhaps Jean will come downstairs and kiss her like before, take hold of a tangle of hair behind her ear and brush his lips against the corners of her mouth, eyes closed, their faces almost not touching. She wants to anticipate, to hear him close to her.

Not that they have forgotten their passion, no. Don't think that they have slumped into marriage as comfort. But she is Italian, prone to passivity. Cavaglià is a memory of seduction, slow, hesitant measures. Heartbeats are counted and heard. She is suffused not with the urge to initiate but only to protect or preserve. And Luc, he has learned somehow to reply.

The echo of sleep, or its approach, begins to sweep down the stairs. Christina decides she should move. She must listen to him, sense if she is able to how he will be in the evening when they are alone, if not follow his direction then surely allow him to suggest. In the café Astrid wiped the streams of spilled chocolate and took away their used cups. The radio rumbled its remains. Cristina was calmer then, while the wondrous duties of motherhood took her and Luc back to her car and the drive to collect Richard, reflecting on the altered quiet in the road noise of open windows. She will go to her office, stall the time with impatient emails about the font, more in demand since its displays on the search engine. Luc will find her when he chooses, as he will.

When Alain's tyre touched the edge of the pavement it was raining, he remembers, or beginning to rain, or about to. L'Homme Rouille was moving his magazines from their racks. There were apples in the footwell of his car, lemons perhaps. No, apples, certainly. He saw the red skin of one as it rolled around. And he had stopped to buy bottles of water for Marie, not knowing.

But the road was wet, he is sure of that. The wheels slipped across the tarmac and led him into the silver Citroën, its driver's eyes closing for the collision. She was dark in the failing light, and blameless. He said so to the police. It was his fault.

There was glass on the road, slices of broken angles from where his bumper had connected with her headlight. The glass glistened in the street lights and L'Homme Rouille's papers were getting wet, so it must have been raining. But there were pedestrians gathered round without umbrellas.

He can recall being surprised at how far back the Citroën had travelled, although he was so focussed on the crash and recoil that he wouldn't be able to tell you exactly what happened. Apples, an apple, rustled the plastic bag and hit Marie's water, he thinks. That was the sound sequence. Impact after impact. Contact, glass, bag, bottle. Or were the bottles on the back seat? Contact, glass, bag, apple? The steering wheel whirled in his hands, instantly tensed. The muscles in his wrists and forearms were sore. If Marie had not left her note, if the following day had been the same as the day before, he would not have been able to draw at work.

His draughtsman's arms, his agile shoulders. Marie loved his shoulders, had told him so many times. Lucy thinks his hands could crush. The Citroën slid backwards and around to the opposite side of the road. Alain saw the driver's face, her dark helplessness. He didn't know that her silver bumper had reached out across the pavement to Maman Sulpice, touching her thigh just gently enough to make her fall.

While the police were there L'Homme Rouille closed his kiosk for the night. Alain watched him walk away, perhaps to a bar to warm himself, perhaps home. 'I've failed your inspection, love, Marie.' His wrists ached. He had stopped to buy her water.

Cristina hears Luc's soft nearing, his shoeless footfall on the landing and the lower stairs. She is typing slowly, pressing each key silently, listening for him, awaiting him. In the kitchen she thinks she hears him stop by the table, imagines him tracing his fingers on the indentations Richard made by banging a cup when he was younger. The wood wears his growth like a landscape, filling its purpose. A family table, for sharing and remembering.

His hands are on her shoulders before she senses he has moved. He leans around her, reading out the few lines she has managed to type. "We are happy to consider your request, if you would provide us with more details," he says. "Anything interesting?"

"A company in Ohio who make gardening equipment. Mowers, chainsaws and hedge cutters, as far as I can tell. They haven't said much so far."

"Do we want his font on the boxes for chainsaws?"

"I don't know. And I'm not sure that's what they want it for."

"What are they offering? We don't really need the money, or Richard doesn't."

"Not at the moment. But maybe we should get what we can for him, while the lettering is still so popular."

"Yes, perhaps." Luc reads the rest of the words on screen, her partial reply. "I like what you've written. Is that what you always say?"

"Not always." She can feel his fingerprints on her, the pressure of his thumbs through her shirt as he leans forwards. She wants to reach her hand up and put it on top of his but the motion is his to make, not hers.

He stands up, releasing his fingers. "We should get somebody else to do this, to answer all these casual enquiries."

"I like it," Cristina replies. "It makes me part of it." He had made the same suggestion before they left. Invisibly she wonders if he is making it again for different reasons, ones which are less concerned with practicality. She misses his touch on her shoulders. Or he might simply have forgotten that he suggested it once before. "Papa and Richard," she adds, as if to explain her connection, and begins to type again, quicker, louder.

"Would you like a drink?" Jean asks. He moves away towards the table and the kitchen beyond it, sensing her need to finish her reply. "Coffee, wine?"

"No thanks." She types. "I'll just do this," she says. And then? What happens once the email has gone and they are alone together? She is nervous in his company. Will they talk again?

"Would you like me to light the fire?" Luc asks.

"It's not cold."

"I know. But would you like me to anyway?" He has to speak, she has to listen. The fire will be her contrition and his.

A waitress at the middle restaurant led Alain to a private table, away from the four other tables already occupied. She was wearing a white shirt and a black skirt. Her dark, helpless hair made her face look rounder than it was. As he waited for Lucie the speaker behind him sang three Brel songs in a row. He knew the first to be *La valse à mille temps*. The second and third he recognised only by the savage sound of the voice. He was close to agony or concern. Lucie was late.

He had given her the name of the restaurant, not its precise location. When she read the title on its canopy she had already walked past it twice, knowing it by another, local name. And it was the place where Jacques had worked, the other Jacques who once had put his hand on her back, outside the cinema. She thought of his attempts at conversation, saw Alain sitting alone at a secluded table.

"I'm late."

"It's all right," Alain lied. "But you've just missed three Brel songs."

"That's good."

"Good that you've missed them?"

"No, that they are playing them. It's his birthday today." She thought of her Jacques, the violence of his teeth, his sweat and saliva, a force, the effort of belief. Her eyebrows and cheeks shaped the language of a loose smile, hidden in attention to the menu placed before her. His passion.

"I've been offered a job in Utrecht."

There are salves available, of course, body lotions devised in Genevese laboratories, combinations of lanolin and glycerine. They promise comfort in essential oils or entice with orchid extracts, vanilla, coconut oil. Some offer peppermint for invigoration, a revitalising blend of almond and raspberries. You could buy simpler options, creams of cocoa butter and mango, tea-tree balms, liniments, essences. Jean-Luc chooses olive oil and tenderness. Sometimes he adds a few crushed leaves of rosemary, for the rich, soothing smell as much as for the sensation on her skin.

She is lying on the sofa again, feeling the loved coolness of the cotton on her feet. Luc waits for her to wriggle into the perfect place then lifts her legs and sits down. His hands are already softened with oil as she rests her feet back on his lap. Silence drifts lightly around them both like a secret.

Her hair is loose. She puts her arm over her face, the back of her wrist pressing into her closed eyes to block out everything but her breathing and his touch, slow and secure. Her legs are too thin. The balls and arches of her soles are sensitive. She is aware that she will flinch if his fingertips catch them too gently. Oil slips around her

151

ankles, the bottom of her calves. He draws his fingers around them, sweeps the trails up to her shins and then down to her feet, makes rhythmical lines and circles as if inscribing her skin. His thumbs smooth minutes into her toes, her heels.

Her eyelids flicker under her wrist like the memory of sleep. In the weak darkness she can still see the hour at the café, is recalling her own voice. She has her image of herself and Luc at the table, her own love or nothing, loss. His hands in motion brush the bottom of her jeans and make them move against her legs, returning her to her physicality.

She can measure from the most basic sound whether someone is Flemish or Dutch, regardless of which language they are speaking at the time. The regions of Italy and France give themselves away in a sigh. Her eyes open, see shades of colour permeating the edges of her arm. Luc is stroking along her instep to the points of her ankles, left foot, right foot, left foot, never letting his skin lose contact with hers.

"It feels like you mean it," Cristina says. She lifts her arm to look at him, watches him concentrate on the flow of oil and her words.

For five days Fabrice has thought about not thinking about Toronto. He has arranged Maman Sulpice's letters into half-conversations the way she had, groups of envelopes locked together by their date and origin. But he has less than half-conversations. He has only the packaging, and that is hidden on his shelves. They are myths, nothing more, stories he knows of but has never heard. The lines of off-white filaments curl at the limits of his vision like the silent gills of Manitoba fungi.

He didn't think of Toronto and he has no one to tell, as he told nobody about it. Perhaps Lucien, when he meets him for dinner. He would at least be excited. And there is a balance, the unobserved and unspoken absence of what might once have been love, or named as such. For five days he has realised. His smile remains.

In the mornings Richard wakes first. The patter of his feet as he runs to the bathroom doesn't wake Cristina. She is tuned to his movements, knows that while she sleeps he will return to his room and play until she goes to him. She doesn't know that first he pushes their door open and looks in, sees their limbs and hair lying in loose curls, like lovers, and we'll sleep safely here.

Lucy arrives at work early, before the evening has fully drifted to darkness. There is a new film and a change of posters, drinks and snack machines to fill, deliveries of stock. Each week the cinema has to remember itself. As she knocks on the glass and waits for Philippe to hear her she can see the shades of the carpet, changed in the last of the natural light. The lines of walking are lighter, worn clean, hold pinks and reds like fresh flowers. Beside those lines are other reds, almost burgundy or brown, fading as the day fades. Soon Philippe will turn on the foyer lights and those above the doors, and all the tones and softness will be lost to the carpet's rough fibres.

"Is he in?" Fabrice asks when he is three steps away, not wanting to surprise her.

She turns. "I think so." Away from the steel and glass it is almost dark.

He sniffs twice, lifting his head as if searching for a source. "We can stay out here, I don't mind waiting." He sniffs again, looks to her for confirmation. "What is that? Violets? Honey?"

Lucy looks up and around, following his example. "I can't smell it."

"Perhaps it's simply the mountains, or the lake," he says, an untethered smile just visible in the grey blue air. "I love Evian, its colours and scents. It's home."

"You're very cheerful."

"Am I? Sorry."

"No, I didn't mean it like that," Lucy says, then sees him twitch his eyebrows to tell her he understood. "Is it because you've finished?"

"No. Yes. Partly." He stumbles to find a way to say that he can't say, and fails. "I don't know." There are still no lights on in the foyer or above the doors but he is happy outside, with the welcoming April night and the nearby sounds of the water. "And you? What did you do while we were closed?"

She hesitates, unsure how to answer, pulls at the hair behind her ear to hear the vibrations of her fingers along the filaments. "Alain's gone."

"Gone?"

"He was offered a promotion, but it meant moving to the Netherlands. He left on Tuesday."

"Lucy, that's so sudden. And sad."

"He asked me to go with him, at dinner on Sunday."

"And are you going to?"

She laughs, half-deliberately. "No."

"You said that very quickly."

"Because I could," she replies, imagining a conversation which was forgiving and pale, perhaps black and white. In the obvious quiet she doesn't prevent the rumour of a smile from appearing as she recalls their meal, Alain's brevity, decisions they had long since made but never spoken out loud.

"I don't know anything about the Netherlands," Fabrice says. The cinema lights are still not on. The glass reflects their images back to them. "No, that's not true," he says, following his thoughts as they swim across to her. He looks at her face for signs of regret, sees the scar on her bottom lip.

The air smells to him of violets or honey, not envelopes. "In the port of Amsterdam there are sailors who sing, of the dreams which haunt them from the shores of Amsterdam," he says, almost singing, letting the words roll to their own rhythm, like water. "That's what I know of the Netherlands. It's an old song. Brel."

"Yes."

Maman Sulpice was buried in a cobalt blue dress with overlays of broderie anglaise around the neck and repaired stitching at the hem. It didn't matter that no one knew why.

About the Author

Simon Holloway is a writer, teacher and researcher based in the UK. Previous work includes short and long fiction, poetry and drama, and he is currently co-writing a critical book on the role of play in the creative process. He currently teaches creative writing at The University of Bolton, has a wife and three sons, and is a firm believer in the wisdom of capybaras.